HONOR BOOK

"Send the woman out, and no one dies."

Parker turned to her. Sienna's blue eyes had widened. Had she remembered her CIA training it would not have taken away her fear, but she would at least know what to do with it. "That's not going to happen." He gripped her shoulder. "I won't give you up to them."

"Maybe you should. They'll kill you otherwise."

"We don't know that."

He knew she wasn't questioning his skills, she was simply concerned for his safety. The warmth of her care over whether he lived or died rushed through him, but there was no time to dwell on it.

"We'll figure a way out."

There was no team within range to help them, but he could call local law enforcement. But would that country sheriff, sixty years old and past ready to retire, live through this? Parker wouldn't be able to stand it if he was responsible for the man being killed or even injured, so he didn't make the call.

He had to find a way to get them out of this all by himself.

D0828772

Lisa Phillips is a British-born, tea-drinking, guitar-playing wife and mom of two. She and her husband lead worship together at their local church. Lisa pens high-stakes stories of mayhem and disaster where you can find made-for-each-other love that always ends in happily-ever-after. She understands that faith is a work in progress more exciting than any story she can dream up. Lisa blogs monthly at teamloveontherun.com, and you can find out more about her books at authorlisaphillips.com.

Books by Lisa Phillips

Love Inspired Suspense

Double Agent
Star Witness
Manhunt
Easy Prey
Sudden Recall

SUDDEN RECALL

LISA PHILLIPS

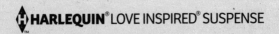

HARLEQUIN® LOVE INSPIRED® SUSPENSE

If you purchased this book without a cover you should be aware
that this book is stolen property. It was reported as "unsold and
destroyed" to the publisher, and neither the author nor the
publisher has received any payment for this "stripped book."

Recycling programs
for this product may
not exist in your area.

LOVE INSPIRED BOOKS

ISBN-13: 978-0-373-67741-2

Sudden Recall

Copyright © 2016 by Lisa Phillips

All rights reserved. Except for use in any review, the reproduction
or utilization of this work in whole or in part in any form by any
electronic, mechanical or other means, now known or hereinafter
invented, including xerography, photocopying and recording, or in
any information storage or retrieval system, is forbidden without
the written permission of the editorial office, Love Inspired Books,
195 Broadway, New York, NY 10007 U.S.A.

This is a work of fiction. Names, characters, places and incidents are
either the product of the author's imagination or are used fictitiously, and
any resemblance to actual persons, living or dead, business establishments,
events or locales is entirely coincidental.

This edition published by arrangement with Love Inspired Books.

® and TM are trademarks of Love Inspired Books, used under license.
Trademarks indicated with ® are registered in the United States Patent
and Trademark Office, the Canadian Intellectual Property Office and in
other countries.

www.Harlequin.com

Printed in U.S.A.

Remember His marvelous works which He has done,
His wonders, and the judgments of His mouth.
—1 Chronicles 16:12

To my readers, thanks for loving all my books so far.
You guys are awesome!

ONE

The beat-up, rusty truck was parked askew on the side of the highway. In the beam of his vehicle's headlights, US Marshal Jackson Parker saw the lone blonde woman kick the flat tire with her black cowgirl boot. He chuckled to himself in the dark of his cab. Sienna did not deal well with feeling incapable, and those lug nuts had probably been tightened by machine.

What was she doing on this lone stretch of highway so late at night, anyway? Her hands were fisted by her sides, halfway covered by the sleeves of a chambray shirt that made her look ordinary when she was anything but. Like she didn't want to be seen. But then why come to his small Oregon town? As far as Parker was concerned, there were limited reasons a CIA agent, or former CIA agent—whichever she was—would want to hide in plain view.

Sienna was either working a job or running away from some kind of trouble.

Parker debated for a second, then pulled over behind her. He left his lights on, since there weren't any streetlamps this far out of town. He was at the tail end of a long night that capped a long day, still in his sweaty clothes and bulletproof vest. The scratch he'd gotten on his face from the fugitive they'd taken down today hurt, but it wasn't bleeding.

Being a marshal was better than climbing through hot jungles and eating sand with every bite, or parachuting into hot zones and barely getting back out alive. Life wasn't exactly boring now that he wasn't a navy SEAL, but at least the job was faster, safer and he could stop for a cheeseburger and large fries on his twenty-minute drive home.

He pulled his tired body from the front seat before he trudged over to her.

"You look like you could use some help." He doubted a person with CIA training was accustomed to needing anything. And yet she'd been bested by a flat tire. He gave her a wry grin.

Her brown eyes were wary. Her blond hair was pulled back in a ponytail, which only served to give him full view of her features.

How was she going to play things this time? Would she continue with the ruse that they didn't know each other, or was she finally going to admit she'd seriously wronged him?

Why persist in giving him no information whatsoever after what they'd shared?

Parker scrubbed his hands down his face. Did he even want to know the answer? He winced when he caught the scratch on his left cheek. "Ma'am?"

"Um…yes. I need help."

"You have a spare?"

She shook her head, a jerky motion. Seriously, now she was scared of him?

Parker folded his arms. "There's no one out here. We're all alone." Her eyes flashed, and she took a step back. Parker gave her a second, but her facial expression didn't change. "Sienna. You can give it up."

"How do you know my name?"

Parker sighed. "You're really going to do this. You don't show up, you don't call, I don't hear from you. Nothing. Then you move to my town and for *a year* I have to deal with you pretending like we don't even know each other. I want to know what's going on, Sienna. None of this makes any sense to me."

"That makes two of us."

He stepped closer. Her eyes widened, and she took a half step back. She was going to have to get over this being-afraid-of-him thing pretty quick. He wasn't the bad guy. Parker leaned down a little and softened his voice. "What's going on? You can tell me."

Maybe this whole thing—being here—was a cover, and he had to go along with it. But it didn't completely ring true. There was definitely something going on. This woman was not your average country girl who lived on a ranch. Not by any stretch.

The last time they'd met, it had been as a CIA agent and a navy SEAL. They'd spent days with each other at one of the forward operating bases in the Middle East, where she'd laid out all the details of his team's mission so they could plan their attack. She'd still been there after it was completed successfully, and they'd been able to tell her that everything she'd informed them about had been spot-on.

It hadn't been a typical set of circumstances. CIA agents generally filed reports, and the intelligence would come down the wires to their SEAL team. But she'd been there herself, recovering from an injury and itching for payback. Parker and his team had been enamored with the lady spy, so tiny but so tough. No one had ever beaten them so badly at pool before, and they'd have let her do it. But she'd whipped them, anyway.

Those few days, before and after, had felt like a vacation to his men. A chance to ease off the stress of consecutive wartime missions. The single guys had tripped over themselves trying to impress Sienna Cartwright, but she'd made it clear Parker was the one who had her attention.

They'd taken things slow. Talked for hours, shared stories of their lives. He'd never told anyone the whole story about his father's illness and what his life had been like. But he'd shared it with her.

And now she acted like she didn't even remember.

Trees drifted in the night breeze. They whooshed against one another like ocean waves. "Someone's coming," she whispered.

They were alone as far as he could tell. If she was in danger or there was some kind of threat, then she of all people knew he was capable of taking care of her.

She hadn't seemed to mind that fact before. She'd actually told him it was one of the things she liked best about him. Despite the fact she was a clearly capable woman, CIA agents had active threats against them. She'd appreciated his ability to defend both of them if need be.

They hadn't said the word *love*, not when it'd been only a matter of days before they were separated. But they'd had plans to meet up later. He'd foolishly thought she meant everything she'd said about caring for him. About wanting to see what the future might hold for them. He'd also unwisely thought she might be different.

But apparently not.

Time had taught him the hard way that women couldn't be trusted. Now his heart wanted an explanation—a seriously good one if she thought she was going to make amends—but that didn't appear to be her plan.

And a woman like Sienna always had a plan.

"Are you in some kind of trouble?"

She peered up at him from beneath her lashes. Her full lips moved like she desperately wanted to say something. Parker's heart was tied in knots, an uncomfortable feeling that resembled the state he'd been in after his wife of four years ran off with his SEAL teammate while the guy was home on leave recovering from an injury. But that was years ago.

Sienna was different than his ex. And not just because she was a spy. So why was she proving, yet again, that he couldn't trust his heart? Maybe all women were like that. But when he looked at her, despite the overwhelming evidence, he just didn't want to believe it.

"Someone is coming," she said again.

Parker glanced around. A vehicle had

crested the hill behind him, headed toward them. "It's just another truck."

Sienna flinched. "They're coming."

"Who?" Parker touched her elbow. "Is someone after you?"

The year of memories Sienna had made since she'd woken up with no knowledge of who she was didn't help her current situation. She had no idea what to do about the giant sweaty guy in front of her who looked like the epitome of the all-American hero. It also didn't help her understand why she was so anxious just because a vehicle was coming down the street toward them.

It was like being inside a tornado while the world swirled around her.

She glanced around and tried to assess the threat. It was something she did instinctually, although what it meant for whom she'd been before she lost her memories she had no idea. Her aunt wouldn't tell her anything, claiming the doctor had instructed her not to for fear she'd cause Sienna to make up memories instead of recalling real things. So instead Sienna had to live with a blank.

And she hated it.

The big guy with the bulletproof vest and the silver-star badge on his belt looked over his shoulder. The van wasn't slowing down. If anything, it'd sped up. When he looked back at her, his features were shadowed.

Was he going to tell her his name?

He knew hers, though how he could've learned it was anyone's guess. Small town, maybe? The handful of times they'd come across each other at the grocery store or the movies—but not at her church, interestingly enough—he only stared at her. Did he think she was some kind of criminal?

The tires on the van squealed and the air filled with the scent of hot rubber. The man with her moved his body between Sienna and the oncoming vehicle, a protective stance she understood but didn't appreciate. Did he think she was helpless? Sienna leaned around him in time to see the side door slide open. Men with guns and black masks jumped out while it was still moving.

Immediately, the man in front of her yanked her arm almost out of its socket as he took off at a run, forcing her to match his punishing pace toward his truck. He pulled her down on the passenger's side and drew his weapon. The fast rat-a-tat of automatic gunfire slammed the metal of his truck, across the hood. He lifted up and returned fire.

More machine-gun fire replied. Air hissed

out of the tire on the far side from where Sienna was hunkered down. Glass shattered in a spray across the pavement.

He pulled her up and shoved her toward the trees. "Plan B. Run!"

Sienna tucked her elbows in and ran into the forest. On her weekend runs, to mix up her workout some, she often ran at this pace for thirty-second spurts just to see if she could. After two minutes now her lungs started to burn. Branches slapped her arms and legs as she sped between trees, and the sound of booted feet pounded the dirt behind her. She glanced back for a second to make sure it was him and not one of those masked men.

Her foot hit something and she stumbled. The man grabbed her arm while she righted herself. "Faster."

Faster? She was almost ready to drop right there and then. Her lungs were about to explode, and he didn't sound much better. Either he had asthma, or…

Sienna looked up at the darkened sky. "Is that a helicopter?" The words came out with each pant of her breath.

He didn't slow down. He glanced behind them, not even losing his stride. "Left." His voice was barely above a whisper.

They angled in that direction toward a tight

collection of bushes. When they reached the copse, he pulled her down. Sienna slammed onto her hands and knees hard enough to leave bruises. Did he have to act like this? Sure, those guys in black were trying to kill them… or him…or just her.

She frowned and whispered, "Why do I feel like I shouldn't be trying to run away from this but should be facing this head-on instead?"

He shook his head and put his finger to his lips.

Was she the kind of person who fought back? She wouldn't have thought so, given how her stomach was roiling. Sienna peeked out of the bushes. Moonlight gave her enough visibility that she could see two figures in the distance make their way toward them. Careful to keep her voice low, she said, "Did you kill one of them?"

"I aimed high, probably just winged him," he whispered. "They were trying to kill us, you know. Instead, they killed my truck." The figures moved closer. "We're going to have to outrun them. One has a camera that is likely thermal imaging. They'll be able to see us hiding."

Thermal imaging? The cover of bushes wouldn't mean anything to someone able to see heat signatures. Sienna and…whatever his name was would be lit up like two beacons.

"Let's go."

She nodded and took his outstretched hand. Going with him was simply the better of the two options. One being death, the other being rescued by a handsome hero. No contest, really. Still, she needed to be careful. She'd been duped by better-looking men than him.

Or at least she thought she might have.

Sienna crept along behind him. How did he make no noise when she seemed to step on every snapping twig in this forest? She should be as good, if not better, than him. Why, she didn't know, but it seemed like that should be a thing. Like she'd learned this, or done this.

But what kind of person knew the best way to run for their life?

Parker glanced up through the trees as the helicopter shone a searchlight over the forest. He angled them to avoid the beam as it swept north to south. His battered body was heavy with fatigue. Old injuries stretched and woke up to let him know they didn't approve of how fast he was moving.

What Parker wanted to know was whether the masked men and the helicopter were here for Sienna or for both of them. It was the first time they'd been alone together. Was that the trigger which had brought this attack down on them? It seemed a long time to wait, a whole year of her living in this town, when these guys could have taken Parker and Sienna out separately. The timing had to mean something.

Maybe she knew the answer. But would she tell him?

He signaled her to split up, circle around and meet back at the road. Halfway through his series of hurried hand motions, she shook her head and whispered, "I don't know what that means."

He wasn't going to explain it. "What's wrong with you?"

The helicopter turned in their direction again. Parker ducked behind a tree and checked the position of the two guys in pursuit. They had dropped back. Were he and Sienna in the clear, or was their retreat a signal things were about to get worse?

She huddled beside him like he was home base. Only this wasn't a game.

Parker said, "Sienna, enough with the act. It's going to get us both killed, so quit pretending you don't know what to do. You're not some untrained civilian, and you need to be all-in or we won't get clear of these guys."

"And I'm supposed to, what, fight them by myself?"

Why was she being so cautious? He wouldn't have signed to her that they should separate if he hadn't known she could handle it.

"I'm not about to help when you're endangering both of our lives by pretending to be helpless." They were almost nose to nose, his voice a hard whisper that sounded scary even to his own ears. But maybe she would listen. Instead, the moonlight glinted off the tears in her eyes. Seriously, now she was going to act like the terrified victim? "Give it up, Sienna."

"Tell me why you know my name. Tell me yours. Tell me anything but that you're going to leave me here to die."

"You know my name."

She shook her head. "I don't know anything. I didn't even know *my* name until Aunt Karen told me."

"You don't have an aunt Karen. You said you had an uncle Bill, but that was it. Or did you lie about that, too, along with everything else?"

Her lip trembled. "Please just tell me your name."

Parker couldn't believe he was actually

going to placate her. "Jackson Parker. Most everyone calls me Parker."

Which she already knew. Only his dad had ever called him Jackson, and he remembered his mom calling him Jack. That was why he only ever told people his name was Parker. He wanted as much separation as possible between who he was now and that scared kid who never thought he'd get away from his lazy, drunk father still pining for a woman who hadn't wanted either of them.

She looked down at the badge on his belt. "A...US marshal?"

He nodded. "Fugitive apprehension task force."

"Am I a criminal?"

"No. Why would you think that?"

"Because I don't know who I am. I have amnesia. I don't remember anything before a year ago, *Parker*. And the year before that I was in a coma."

Amnesia? Parker stared at her, dumbfounded.

She was looking at him like maybe he could help her sort this out.

The reality was, he probably could. He had to get them out of this first before he unraveled the loose threads in her stories. If she was lying—again—he'd find out sooner or later, and he'd know never to trust her or any other woman. Ever.

If she wasn't lying, Parker wouldn't stop until he got to the bottom of what had happened to her. Something had turned the strong, capable woman he'd known into the scared and shaking one in front of him. And he was going to find out what.

He took her hand again and started walking. The helicopter was overhead still. Parker cut right, then left, then right again, working his way back to the road. Why had he left his cell phone in the cup holder in his truck?

He needed to call this in, get his whole team here to battle these guys. Making arrests, interrogating suspects and seeing justice done was his life now.

As for Sienna, he didn't know what her life entailed. None of this made any sense, except her not being able to remember who she was. Amnesia actually fit everything he'd seen so far, but how could that have happened? A *year* in a coma? Where was the CIA now? Even harmless and unable to go on missions, surely they kept tabs on an asset like her.

Parker had a lot of questions. The first of which was where those two men had gone.

He slowed his pace and listened as Sienna quieted her breaths. Some things were still there. The way she reacted, the way she scanned the vicinity around her. Training had been ingrained in her until it was muscle memory, even as freaked out as she was and with no past.

His Sienna was still in there, and maybe she'd be able to tell him why she had left him standing by himself at the airport in Atlanta. Why she'd promised to be there and then hadn't shown. He'd been fresh off that last mission and anxious to see her—to see where their relationship might go when they were both stateside with some time off.

The timing of her no-show at the airport didn't fit the "coma" she'd been in. If it'd lasted a year, it would have begun weeks, or even a month, after she stood him up. There had to be another reason she had never showed. Once Parker knew what it was, he'd be able to walk away without this twisting thing in his chest that wouldn't let him rest. She'd torn him up inside, but he'd given her the power to do that first. No more. He wasn't going to give his heart to another woman, ever. He was done with that.

Sienna gasped, and the hot barrel end of a rifle touched Parker's neck. He had to think quickly. In one maneuver he twisted and went for the rifle.

The shot slammed into his chest.

TWO

Sienna looked back at Parker, lying on the ground. Was he dead? She couldn't see any blood, but it was dark. The air had chilled until her breath puffed out around her in white clouds. She was dragged by her arm back through the forest the way they came by a masked gunman.

The helicopter had quit circling with that blinding light and landed, probably on the road. Were they going to chopper her out? They could certainly try. Sienna might be an amnesia patient who'd been in a coma for a year, but she wasn't going to go down without a fight.

Where was all this bravado coming from? She hadn't been completely idle this past year. She had a working knowledge of self-defense, more for the sake of meeting people and getting out of the house to attend classes. But otherwise, her life had been quiet. Pleasant.

Yet now, fear seemed to have distilled inside her like some weird Frankenstein-type science experiment. In its purest element she was left with something rock hard and unwavering. Like the all-American hero's forearms.

Sienna glanced at the man on the other side of her, covering her with his Eastern European ex-military rifle and those Russian surplus thermal goggles hanging loose around his neck. Most of that was available to buy on the internet, which meant these guys could be anyone and not necessarily just hired guns of the nasty variety...and *how* did she know that? She grew vegetables and raised goats for milk. How did she know where those items had come from?

The rifle was lifted for a second, just long enough for her to get the message. Apparently, trying to run was out of the question. So what was the new plan? And was Parker dead?

"We figured sooner or later you'd go to him for help. Little obvious, don't you think? Crying to the big bad SEAL in his cushy new job driving prisoners around. Too bad he can't help you no more. Too, too bad."

Sienna swallowed. Tears filled her eyes, and that painful ache in her chest was back. It usually only surfaced after a bad dream—like the one she had of that little boy crying. She didn't even know Parker, despite his apparently thinking they were best friends or something. Why would she shed a tear over the death of someone she barely knew?

Still, it slipped down her face, and she didn't wipe it away in case the gunmen were watching. They'd let down their guard if they thought she was as helpless as she looked.

She kept up her act when the gunman's grip on her arm tightened just enough that she could reasonably let off a whimper. They'd soon think she was surrendering, but her first order of business was getting out of his hold. Then she'd either have to steal their van or run down the street until she found someone willing to give her a ride into town.

They stepped out of the trees and the helicopter's rotors whipped her hair around her face, obstructing her view of the three vehicles and the man holding his arm. Parker had been right; he'd winged one of the gunmen.

"I can't believe you let him hit you." The rifleman to her right lifted his weapon, his voice disappointed but in a hard way. There was no sympathy for his friend.

"It was a mistake. I won't let it happen again." The injured man spoke in broken English.

"You're right, you won't." The rifle popped off one shot, and the injured man fell to the ground.

Sienna looked away from the carnage while the rifleman chuckled.

"Let's go." The man holding her stepped over the dead guy, which forced her to do the same. "You have an appointment with the boss."

"I think you have the wrong person. This must be some mistake. I run a tiny ranch and I take care of my sick aunt. What could you possibly want with me?"

"Not us, just the boss." He chuckled. "Nice try, though. This whole 'I don't remember' act is cute and all. I nearly busted a gut when I heard about that. But it's not going to fly. The boss has ways of making people remember things."

Dread crested over her like an ice cold wave. She wasn't going to suddenly get her memories back, not even with whatever horrifying method their "boss" came up with. The doctors couldn't do anything about her amnesia, which was why she'd checked out of the hospital.

A year later and she still didn't recall one iota of her past. Aunt Karen asked her about it every few weeks, but other than that she just let Sienna go about her business.

The whole thing was bizarre. And not just the situation she was in now.

Aunt Karen was like an acquaintance living in her house. Sienna had figured she'd develop familial affection for the older woman at some point, but it hadn't happened yet. What kind of niece didn't even love her own aunt? And what had Parker said, about her not even having an aunt, just an uncle? How strange was that?

It was like everyone knew more about her life than she did. Sienna wanted to grab her hair at the roots. All the tiptoeing around, all the side glances and making sure she hadn't snapped. It was infuriating. She wanted to just get in her truck—if it actually worked— and drive off into the sunset. But every time she got ready to leave, it was like her aunt got needier.

Now she was about to get a ride out of town when she really didn't want to go.

The gunman shook her arm. "Move. Now."

Parker was pretty sure his rib was broken. He lay on the ground listening to the men walking Sienna to the van, then rolled over and did a push-up, getting his legs under him. *Oh, that hurt.* He jogged after them in time to see her struggle against the man holding her, desperate not to be put on the waiting chopper. *Good girl.*

She was giving the fight a valiant effort, further proof that what she'd said was true. In fight-or-flight mode no one was good enough to keep up the pretense. She'd have done even better in this situation had she retained all of her previous skills, which meant they likely truly had been forgotten.

At least these men didn't seem to want her dead, or she'd have been killed already. No, they only wanted him dead—which was pretty much the story of his life.

Since the single gunman had his back to him, Parker cracked the door on his truck and grabbed his phone, hoping they wouldn't see the dome light. He sent a text to the duty phone at the marshal's office that was manned 24/7, a code that meant, "Get everyone here. I'm in serious trouble," along with his location. The team wouldn't thank him given they'd also had a rough day, and were probably all home in bed by now. But they would understand.

Parker clicked the door as quietly as he could while Sienna kicked and struggled against her captor.

The helicopter pilot yelled through the open door. "Let's go!"

Parker took cover behind the truck, his gun aimed at the man. "US Marshals—let her go!"

The gunman pointed his weapon and fired. Parker ducked for a second, then lifted up to shoot again—aiming for the far side of the man so there was less chance a miss would hit Sienna.

She kicked out at the gunman so that the man's shots went wide and missed Parker. Sienna grabbed the man's head and ripped the wool balaclava from his face.

Brown hair fell down across his forehead and surprise flashed on his face, distracting him enough that Sienna was able to slam his head back against the side of the helicopter. He dropped to the concrete, unconscious. *Maybe she hasn't forgotten everything.*

A boot crunched gravel at his back and Parker spun. He sideswiped the rifle with his forearm and punched the man. The fight was nasty, but Parker got him on the ground, arms behind his back. "Who sent you here?"

The man didn't answer.

Sienna sprinted over and took cover behind Parker.

Parker asked again, "Who sent you?"

The man on the ground chuckled. The words he spoke were Italian, but Parker understood them nonetheless. He was going to kill himself. Before Parker could flip the man to his back and prevent the suicide, he'd already bitten down on what was likely a cyanide capsule in a fake tooth.

Parker pulled Sienna away so she didn't have to see or hear the man's unpleasant death. The helicopter rotors spun faster and it lifted off the ground, those inside apparently fully prepared to cut their losses and bail on this whole endeavor.

Parker held his arm around their faces while wind flicked his shirttails up and down. A convoy of cars pulled up and parked in the spot where the helicopter had been, surrounding the remaining living man. His team piled out, guns drawn, looking as perturbed as he felt.

Parker turned Sienna so she could focus on him. "Are you okay?"

She nodded. "Thank you."

He wanted to say, "Always," but that would imply there was some kind of link between them, some emotional connection deeper than two strangers standing by a truck on a highway. He wasn't going there again; he had to keep a distance.

"You want to tell us what on earth is going on, Parker?" His boss, Jonah Rivers, was newly married and probably mad he'd been pulled away from precious time with his bride.

Behind Jonah was US Marshal Wyatt Ames, a former police detective, and behind him the team's married couple—Hailey and Eric Hanning. Jonah's gaze was riveted on the front of Parker's vest.

Parker glanced down and saw the bullet lodged there. Jonah's eyebrow rose.

"Everyone, this is Sienna."

Ames grinned, but then he always was cocky. "Explains a few things."

Parker ignored him and pointed out everyone so she knew their names. "I was with Sienna when she was almost abducted by this guy." He pointed at the man who'd killed himself with the capsule in his tooth. "And this guy." He pointed at the man who'd been shot, though Parker was only responsible for the graze on his arm. "The one over there is only unconscious."

Eric and Hailey broke off to handcuff the last man alive.

Parker blew out a breath while Jonah strode over and held out his hand. "It's good to see you, Sienna."

Parker whipped his head around. "You know her?"

Sienna said, "I watched some of the zoo animals at my ranch after the flood, up until Jonah's wife, Elise, reopened it a month ago."

"That was you?"

"Yes." There was a question in her eyes. "My aunt didn't like it, either, but I told her it wasn't like the animals were going to come in the house, so why should she be bothered by them?"

"That's how I met Sienna."

Parker didn't like the smug look on Jonah's face. He wanted to tell his boss everything he knew about Sienna's past—her real past and not whatever story she'd concocted instead of telling people the truth about her bizarre medical case. Then he'd watch Jonah's facial expression change.

Instead, Parker said, "How nice."

Jonah chuckled, apparently not fazed by Parker's belligerence. He never was, and Parker hadn't been hired on to a fugitive apprehension task force because of his people skills.

"I'm assuming the helicopter reported in this area was on account of you?"

While Parker told Jonah all about what had happened, Sienna left him and strode to her truck. Her purse was still on the front seat, her phone inside. Nothing had been taken, which made sense since the gunmen hadn't been there for that. They'd been there for her, and when they'd failed, the one in charge had...

killed himself. Who did that? Her mind spun so fast she was dizzy from it.

Sienna had twenty-three texts and three voice mails from her aunt. She sent a text back that said, I'm fine.

Two seconds after it sent, her phone rang. She turned to sit sideways on the front passenger seat and answered.

"Yes."

"Where are you? I've been calling you for an hour!"

Sienna gritted her teeth. "I got a flat tire, then three men with guns and a helicopter chased me through the forest and I barely got free before they could put me in the chopper and take me to who knows where."

Silence. "Did you kill them?"

Sienna choked. She'd said the whole thing in her most sarcastic voice, like what happened was just another day at the office, and Aunt Karen only wanted to know if Sienna had killed them? "Two of them are dead, but it wasn't me who did it."

Why was her aunt worried about that, and not whether or not Sienna was okay? Because while she was fine physically, mentally was a whole other question. "Listen, Aunt Karen, I'll be home soon to heat up dinner…"

"I already ate. Is someone there with you?"

"A marshal stopped to help me with the flat."

"Jackson Parker?"

Sienna frowned. "How did you know that?"

"Have him drive you home. Tell him to come inside so I can meet the man who saved my darling niece's life."

It just didn't ring true. Nothing about her life did except the feel of Parker's hand wrapped around hers. Remembering it was keeping her sane when she wanted to drop to the ground and cry. Not just from fear. When she looked at Parker it was like all those feelings of loss surrounding what she couldn't remember intensified.

Maybe he was right and they had been friends. She wasn't big on trusting people on face value, but Parker made her want to believe it. It felt right. *He* felt right.

But there was nothing she could do about it when she didn't recall a thing. She couldn't make any kind of move when she didn't know their history. What if there was something huge she was missing because she'd lost her past? If she jumped in now, she'd look naive. That was why she had to back off and not rely on Parker too much, even if it was the easy route.

Sienna hung up and rubbed her gritty eyes. When she looked up, one of the marshals was in front of her. He shot her a cocky grin and stuck his hand out. "Wyatt Ames."

She shook it. "Sienna Cartwright." As always, it sounded foreign. Like she was living someone else's life.

"So you're the one who has him all tied up in knots."

"Excuse me?"

"Parker." Wyatt glanced once in his direction and then back at her. "A man doesn't look at a woman like that if it doesn't mean something."

"Am I supposed to know what you're talking about?"

He grinned. "I guess not. Parker told us about the amnesia thing. That really happens?"

Sienna kept a straight face. "I wouldn't know. I can't remember."

Wyatt laughed, which made Parker pause in his conversation and look over at her. "That's exactly the look I'm talking about."

Parker went back to his conversation, and Sienna shook her head. "It's not like that. We barely know each other."

Well, she barely knew *him*. The reverse might not be true.

"Listen, I really need to…"

She was interrupted when the gunman she'd knocked out started yelling as he regained consciousness. Parker raced over while the marshals struggled to restrain him. Sienna watched, wide-eyed, as he stuck two fingers in the gunman's mouth. The man bit down. Parker winced but didn't back off. He pulled out a capsule and lifted the man up. "Put this one on suicide watch."

The female marshal nodded, and they hauled the guy to their car.

Parker walked to her then, giving Wyatt a side nod that made him stride away. But not before he glanced back at Sienna and mouthed, *See.*

She wasn't interested in getting mixed up in the interplay between the marshals. That wasn't her world. All she wanted was to get back to the ranch and hide under her covers until the sun came up.

"Are you okay?" The hardness of Parker's features had softened. She steeled herself against it and glanced at the trees. That persistent feeling of being watched just wouldn't go, even now that the immediate threat had passed.

"I'm not sure how I'm going to get home."

"At last, a problem of yours I can actually solve." The smile curled the corners of his mouth. "I'll give you a ride. Okay?" Sienna nodded, and Parker strode past Wyatt, who handed him a set of keys. She glanced again at the dark forest around them as she followed. There was definitely someone out there.

THREE

With the exception of telling him where she lived, Sienna had been quiet on the drive to her house. He'd tried to fill the silence with music and found out the painful way that Wyatt had changed all the radio stations to what he called "classics." Parker wanted to reach over and hold her hand, but to her they were practically strangers.

Instead, he squeezed the steering wheel until he worried it would snap.

"Is there something wrong?"

He glanced over but couldn't see her expression in the dark of the SUV Wyatt had loaned him. "It's been a long day."

"Oh, sorry I kept you out."

"Not your fault." He snapped on his blinker and turned onto her street. "You didn't ask those men to try and kidnap you."

She turned away and looked out the window. The clock on the dash read 11:37 when he pulled into her drive next to a van. "Is that your aunt's car?"

"It's supposed to give her the feeling of mobility by allowing her to get out on her own, but she doesn't like to drive so I still have to take her everywhere."

He didn't hear any resentment in her voice, just fatigue. Which after the night she'd had, running through the forest and fighting for her life, didn't surprise him. "Was she in an accident?"

Sienna nodded. "It was before I woke up with no memory. She doesn't really talk about it, but I found a newspaper article online. A drunk driver hit her car late at night, and now she's paralyzed from the waist down. She has a nurse come in every morning to help her shower and dress, but I help her the rest of the time."

Parker didn't know what to say, so he cracked the door and climbed out. A light over the porch flooded the front of the house with its fluorescent glare. Not a motion sensor. That would have been triggered by the vehicle pulling in. A heat sensor, then? Not many small-town residents had security like that. Parker wanted to meet this aunt of hers.

He waited for Sienna to circle the SUV and then took her hand. Because he wanted to. Because they were both tired, and they could have died tonight. It wasn't about what he wished could have been, or what they might have had between them had she shown up in Atlanta. It was only about providing the comfort of friendship when they'd both had a bad day.

The front steps had been overlaid with a wood ramp. When Parker stepped his foot on it, a buzzer inside dinged—like a doorbell. They reached the front door just as it swung open to reveal a stout woman in a wheelchair.

With dark hair plastered on her head, she looked like a stern schoolmarm. A fact that was confirmed when she stuck her fingers on her hips and barked, "Took you long enough to get home. Did you get lost?"

Sienna grabbed a gray cardigan from a hook inside the door and pulled it on over the shirt she wore, like armor. "Sorry, Aunt Karen. We got here as soon as we could. Why don't you head to bed? We've all had a long day." She rubbed her hands up and down her arms.

The woman chuckled, an awkward, rusty sound. "You look more than worse for wear. Are you going to introduce me to your friend?"

Like she didn't know exactly who he was? Because he'd met her before under entirely different circumstances. And *he* knew she was

CIA. Why was she acting like this was a cover story for a mission?

Karen glanced at Parker, and he lifted an eyebrow in question. Then "Aunt Karen" pinned him with a stare Sienna didn't catch and shook her head. Did she think she was fooling anyone? Parker wasn't sure why he was willing to go along with it, but if there was a chance it was for Sienna's benefit, he would.

At least until he got an explanation as to why Sienna's CIA handler was here, pretending to be her relative.

Karen glanced between them. "How about I make us some tea? Why don't you take a hot shower, get warmed up? Your young man and I can get acquainted."

Sienna glanced at him.

Parker wasn't going anywhere right then.

She sighed. "Okay, that actually sounds good. I'll be back down in a minute."

"You take your time." Karen wheeled herself into the kitchen.

The corner of Sienna's mouth curled up. "She's a little…abrasive, but her bark is worse than her bite."

"That's good to know." Parker squeezed her shoulder. "I'll be fine. I'm a big tough guy who fights off kidnappers, remember?"

It was supposed to be a joke, but he knew she didn't take it that way when her eyes darkened. "I remember."

"Sorry." He took a step of retreat toward the kitchen. "I'll make small talk while you clean up."

She cocked her head to the side. "Why are you staying? It's late, and you're more tired than I am."

He couldn't tell her that "Aunt Karen" had some explaining to do. So he said, "I don't want to leave right away if there's a chance they might come back. I'll stick around for a little while and then head out. If that's okay with you."

She nodded. Honestly, she looked relieved. But Parker didn't let that sink too far down. His heart didn't need any more encouragement. Sienna turned to the hall and left him alone in the foyer.

Karen rolled to the doorway. "Kitchen. Now."

Parker followed because it was the only way he was going to get answers.

The phone on the counter rang.

Karen grabbed the wheels of her chair.

"I'll get it!" Sienna's yell came from down the hall.

Karen shook her head and turned back to Parker.

"Seriously?" was all he said as he folded his arms and leaned his hips against the kitchen counter while he waited for Karen to give him some kind of answer for all of this. Sienna was out of earshot at least, on the phone by the sound of it. That meant he could talk freely with her "aunt."

The older woman pinned him with a stare. It was no less effective, though he and Karen were no longer on the same eye level as when he'd last seen her two years ago. "I'm not going to tell Sienna who she really is. And you can't, either."

"What happened to you?"

"I was hit by a drunk driver. Sienna didn't tell you? It happened while she was in a coma, so when she woke up, it was decided that I would stay with her."

Parker said, "You're lying about being her aunt so you can be here when she remembers whatever it is the CIA wants her to recall?"

"Yes." There was no guilt in Karen's expression, but then there never had been. Nor any pity when she'd found him in a sorry state just days after Sienna's no-show. The day she'd stiffly told him to drop it, to let Sienna be and to go on with his life. To forget about her, like he could do that. Like there was no hope a CIA agent and a SEAL could find happiness together.

"What did Sienna forget that is so important?"

Sienna grabbed the phone off the desk. "Hello?"

The landline was down the hall in the office, where Aunt Karen holed up most of the day working on what she called her "correspondence." Sienna figured she just read romance novels, given how many paperback books regularly showed up in the mail.

A sigh of relief was the first thing she heard. "Are you okay?"

"Uh…yes." Sienna didn't question the need; she simply strode to the door and clicked it shut without any sound.

"I can't believe you're actually okay."

Who was this woman?

Sienna let the towel drop to the desk. "Why do I want to cry right now?"

"Because I'm the person who you love more than anything in the world, and we haven't talked to each other in nearly two years."

Sienna was sort of over other people knowing who she was. "Why would I love you? What's so special about you?"

The woman on the phone laughed, took a long inhale and then laughed some more.

Sienna set her hand on her hip. "Seriously, I want to know."

She chuckled, wheezing for breath. "That's my girl. Don't believe anything they tell you. At best, it's nothing but a bunch of half-truths."

"And at worst?"

"You're not ready for that."

"Is Sienna Cartwright even my real name?"

The woman was silent for a minute. "It was your birth name, but you've had so many aliases I can imagine it sounds weird."

"And what did I call you?"

"Oh, right. Amnesia." She chuckled again. Did people really laugh that much? "I'm Nina. Nina Holmes, your best friend since third grade."

It couldn't be a coincidence. Sienna had been living here months, and tonight she'd almost been kidnapped. Now this woman was on the phone, claiming to be her friend? Did this "Nina" think that she would buy it?

"Prove it. Because if you were my best friend, you wouldn't have waited two years to contact me," Sienna said.

"I was instructed not to. And there isn't much I'm allowed to tell you—even if I seriously disagree with the reason. But...you take honey in your coffee."

"What else?"

Nina was quiet for a second. "Oh, I have a good one. Your favorite dessert."

It had taken Sienna two months of experimenting with different varieties to figure out the answer to that one for herself. For some reason it had been important to get it right. "If you think you can answer."

"A scoop of strawberry ice cream and a scoop of chocolate—which is gross when you stir them together, by the way—with broken-up pieces of peanut-butter cups you hide in the freezer."

Okay, so that was pretty specific. "And on top…?"

"A cherry. Obviously. No whipped cream. Which is also bizarre."

Sienna smiled. More than anyone she'd met since she woke up from the coma, Sienna believed this woman actually knew her. Not that she thought Karen or Parker were lying, but deep affection welled up in her at hearing this woman's voice. She knew she could reach out to Nina, but she still had to be cautious.

"Will they try to kidnap me again?"

It was a test, but she had to know what Nina knew.

"My guess, yes. They were hired, and since

the first team failed, he's likely going to hire another team to try again."

So many questions popped into Sienna's head, but she focused on the most pressing. "He?"

"I don't know his name," Nina said. "You're the only one who did."

"What does this man want with me?"

Nina was quiet for a moment. "He wants you to remember."

"Does he think I don't want the same thing? It's all I've wanted for a year now. It's all anyone wants." Sienna squeezed her eyes shut. "Why is this such a big deal?"

"You're not ready for that, either."

"Well, you have to give me something, because I feel like I'm going crazy!"

Sienna took a breath to pray Aunt Karen and Jackson Parker hadn't heard her. The last thing she needed was for them to look at her like she was something to be pitied. That wasn't who she was. She was a fighter. How else would she have lasted living this long in a cloud of confusion with no way out and not go crazy?

"I can give you a way out of that house, but that's all I can do. Karen was right about one thing, you do have to remember on your own."

"How do you know she told me that?"

"It was the plan." Nina paused. "Do you

want an out or not? Because I'm in your neighborhood, so if you want space to figure this out I can help you. I'll pick you up."

Sienna wanted to say yes. She wanted to jump at the chance to see this woman she was clearly deeply connected to, if the way her chest was twisting was any indication. Did people really feel like that about those they were closest to? She might have that with Parker, if she allowed herself to find out how deep the well of her feelings for him went. And if they really did know each other like he claimed.

But something about Nina told her their bond had been forged through weathering hard times together. The kind of connection lifelong friends have. A bond that surpassed a blank memory. Her heart knew this woman, just like her heart knew Parker. But which one did she choose?

"This offer has a time limit. I'm not supposed to be here, but I received word from a contact that something was going down tonight. By the time I got to the scene, I heard the suspects were either dead or had already been arrested and you'd escaped. So I came to see if you needed anything."

"I appreciate that."

"But you don't want to come?"

"I need answers. Coming with you isn't going to give them to me any more than staying here will."

Nina said, "Then I suggest you take another look at that shoebox you have under your bed."

Karen calmly took a sip of her coffee. "Sienna hid something."

Parker ignored his. "What happened to her?"

"You mean why did my best asset wind up in a coma for a year before she woke up with no memory of who and what she is?" Karen tutted. "She was supposed to retrieve some merchandise and switch it out with a fake so that the seller didn't pass on anything sensitive when he made the sale. We think she made the switch, realized she was in danger and hid the original. Somehow the seller found out he had a fake and gave Sienna to the buyer so he could get the location out of her."

A second of silence was the only indication Karen felt anything for Sienna's well-being. "The extraction team found her unconscious in a bathtub of water. She told you the rest."

Parker's mouth went dry. He tried to swallow. "Is this the reason she didn't meet me?"

Karen shook her head like it was a dumb question, but Parker didn't regret asking. She said, "It was weeks between you and this mission. The two are unrelated."

"And yet Sienna, and you, are here. In my town. Why is that?"

"It's because of her."

Parker didn't say anything. How had she known to come here?

"She was convinced this was where she lived. For whatever reason—" Karen eyed him, like it was his fault "—she had some kind of tie to this place. I found her staring at a map online, trying to see if anything looked familiar. This is where she picked." Karen paused. "Out of the entirety of the continental United States, Sienna picked the tiny town where *you* live. I could hardly tell her she was wrong when she was so convinced she should come here."

Parker didn't want to gloat, but it was hard to hold it back. He'd told her at length about his hometown. As a woman with little to no geographical ties, she'd soaked it up.

"I see."

Karen glared.

"I'm sorry about your injuries."

She sniffed. "It's not as bad as it looks, but it did serve a purpose. Sienna has had plenty of time to remember who she was."

"But she hasn't, and now someone tried to kidnap her. You think it's the buyer or the seller?"

Karen shrugged.

"Who are they?"

"We're not sure. Sienna knew. We're blind on this one until they make enough of a move that we can find out who they are. We're tracking the chopper, but the two dead and the one in your custody had no IDs and no cell phones on them. One had a British military insignia tattoo, but aside from that we have no clue as to their identities."

Parker wasn't even going to ask how the CIA knew anything about the men from the scene. Whatever his team learned from the man in custody, the CIA had discovered minutes later. But if it protected Sienna, who was he to complain?

"So what did Sienna intercept? What was this 'seller' trying to pass off?"

"That's classified information, and until I get a reply as to your security clearance, I can't tell you much more than I have. Suffice it to say, what she hid was highly sensitive. It cannot fall into the wrong hands."

"You realize I won't leave this alone."

Karen sighed. "I was afraid of that."

"I was there. I saw the danger she was in, and they knew me. I'm convinced they did. Likely now they'll think Sienna and I are working together. It may even be why they moved in."

"They moved in because they found her."

"Then she needs to be relocated. Immediately." Parker would book vacation days and sign up for that detail first thing tomorrow... from a highway two states away, if that's what it took to keep Sienna safe.

His heart was tied up in this. It was impossible to deny that fact. When Sienna remembered who she was and who they were to each other, then he'd know where he stood. Until then, there was nothing he could do about that. But he could keep her safe.

Karen sent him her stern schoolmarm look again. "The CIA are the ones calling the shots in this, Jackson Parker. Not you."

The gasp was audible. Parker turned and saw Sienna in the hallway, her eyes wide.

"The CIA?"

FOUR

Sienna stood frozen in the kitchen doorway. Why hadn't she just gone to her bedroom— to the shoebox under her bed that Nina had told her about? She should be in the shower. Anywhere, doing anything other than being slammed with information.

Something in that shoebox was important enough that Nina thought it would help Sienna figure this out or at least provide answers on something. But she wasn't in her room, looking through it. No, Sienna had given in to the curiosity of knowing whether Parker was still here.

"The CIA?"

Karen didn't move.

"Am I really supposed to believe the CIA has something to do with me?"

Karen's face was flat. Like always. "You are supposed to remember on your own. The doctor said…"

"That you can't just tell me. I know." Sienna

bit down hard. "I guess now I know why." She turned to leave the room while her thoughts spun like some amusement park ride. But there was nothing fun about this.

"Sienna, don't walk away!"

She turned back to her aunt, who was now red faced. She probably shouldn't be getting worked up. Sienna doubted that was good for her health. But she didn't know, because Karen never talked about it.

She lifted her hands and let them fall to her sides. "Am I supposed to be, what…freaked out? Because I am. Seriously? The CIA? I'm very curious why you think the Central Intelligence Agency is relevant here. Because as far as I can see, I have nothing to do with spies or any of that."

Karen didn't say anything.

"That's it? You drop a bomb and you have nothing to say?" Sienna waited, but her aunt still didn't offer up anything. "Not even to confirm or deny?"

Even Parker said nothing, intently watching the interplay between Sienna and her aunt.

This whole night had been like the bad dreams she had. Dreams where she fought against an unknown attacker who was bigger and stronger. She always woke drenched in sweat and out of breath—like she'd been fighting for her life. But the question lingered. Had it been real, a memory or simply a dream?

The CIA and a fight to the death?

"Now I know why you didn't want to tell me."

Karen flinched. "I wasn't allowed."

"Someone tried to kidnap me tonight. If the CIA is part of it I'm obviously in danger. And you thought the best course of action was to keep this information from me? When knowing would have kept me safe, instead of putting me in danger."

"Deputy Marshal Parker was there."

"He was shot." Sienna felt hot tears gather in her eyes. "If he hadn't been wearing his vest, he would be dead right now."

Sienna took a step back. Not a retreat, more of a calculated move to give her time to re-formulate her plan. Everything had changed tonight. Her. Nina. Parker. Karen. The foundation of her life had shifted, leaving her adrift and trying to grasp something steady to hold on to.

She slipped her fingers in her front pocket to grasp the folded paper that she'd kept there every day since she left the hospital. She'd never told anyone about the verse she had found in her own handwriting on a tiny folded strip of paper tucked in her wallet.

The only real connection to her past.

"I'm going to take that shower. Too much has happened tonight. I need time to process before I can decide what I'm going to do next."

Karen's eyebrows rose. "Next? You aren't going to do anything but stay here. Until you start to remember, you can't leave."

Parker's voice was low and lethal. "And exactly what will happen if she does leave?"

Sienna had thought Karen's words a veiled threat, also. Was her aunt going to give a straight answer this time?

"I only meant I need her here."

Did she really? There was a whole lot below the surface to Aunt Karen that she wasn't sharing. Meanwhile, Sienna was expected to give regular updates as to what she might be remembering and what was only her imagination while she slept. Like Karen was some kind of licensed psychotherapist.

The CIA?

Sienna's life had taken a bizarre turn. She didn't want to even think about whether or not that might be true. She wanted her quiet life. She *liked* her quiet life. Aunt Karen's declaration was a disturbance. Jackson Parker's presence was a gigantic disruption she wasn't comfortable with at all. She didn't need him, and he could take care of himself. But when those warm blue eyes stared at her, she couldn't help feeling there was something more between them she was supposed to remember.

Friends, he'd said. But she wanted to rush to him, to bury her face in his chest and let him hold her. Was that the type of friends he was talking about? She couldn't help but wonder if he hadn't been more than that to her.

That was why he was so dangerous to her peace of mind.

She needed to remember the truth about her past, not be distracted by the possibility of a romance that may or may not have been. What if he'd wanted to be friends and she'd wanted more? That would be humiliating to remember.

She shot him a look. "You should probably be going. It's late."

She was dismissing him. Parker had hoped that when the truth came out, she would seek his help. Trust him to keep her safe through whatever this was. He didn't want the man who'd sent that team to kidnap her to try again, but he had to consider the possibility they wouldn't stop.

Parker didn't want to stop, either, and he didn't want to leave.

She'd ditched him for her job and then gone

and gotten herself hurt. But his heart couldn't get past waiting at that airport for her—and coming to terms with the fact that she wasn't going to show up. She might need him, but she didn't want him.

He pushed off the counter. "I'll go, if that's what you want me to do."

Karen's eyes widened, but Parker didn't care if she was surprised by him. He was only doing what Sienna wanted.

He crossed the space between where he stood and Sienna. The phone on the counter rang. Parker swiped it up in frustration as he passed and barked out a "Hello?"

Sienna's jaw dropped. In a cartoon, this would have been where smoke poured from her ears along with a whistling sound.

"Oh, great," the woman said. "It's *you.*"

"Excuse me?"

The female voice on the phone laughed. "The boy-wonder navy SEAL now a deputy-marshal-famous-fugitive-catcher. I did my homework. Don't think I don't know everything about you. And don't underestimate me."

Parker fought the urge to smile. "Is that supposed to be intimidating?"

"Just promise me you're going to keep her

safe." The woman sighed. "If she won't leave with me, then I need you to make sure she's okay."

Sienna was supposed to have left, to be protected by this woman? If Parker had to guess, he figured this must be Sienna's best friend. He looked at Sienna then. She motioned frantically for him to give her the phone. She did look sort of guilty—about the fact that she'd considered ditching him and meeting up with her friend, maybe?

Parker didn't give up the phone. "Tell me, why does Sienna need your help?"

If this woman had more information than what Karen had told him, then he wasn't going to overlook her as a source. Or an ally. Too bad he couldn't remember what her name was. Natalie…Nellie. Something like that.

The woman said, "They want whatever she hid from them. Karen wouldn't tell me what it was, just that Sienna doesn't remember anything, least of all where she hid it. They *will* try and abduct her again, and then they'll torture her for its location before they kill her. But if she doesn't even remember who she is, or what it is, then how can she tell them? I don't even want to think what they'll try in order to jog her memory. Last time, when the CIA found her, she was barely alive."

"Understood."

Sienna stepped closer. "Give me the phone, Parker."

He shook his head and then turned away. "Can we trust you?"

"Are you willing to risk her life if I'm not telling the truth?"

"No."

"Then yes, you can."

Karen's eyes narrowed. "Who are you talking to?"

Parker tucked the receiver under his chin. "I don't know her, but she knows who I am."

"Nina." Karen didn't seem to think much of this mystery caller.

He turned his attention back to the call. "Anything else I should know?" He wanted to ask this "Nina" about Karen, but not when she was in the room.

"Just don't let anything happen to Sienna. I'll help when I can." She paused. "Give me your number."

Parker rattled it off, happy to accept an ally in this. Even if he didn't know her. Sienna had told him enough the first time they met.

"Got it." Nina hung up.

"Stay in touch." Parker set the phone back

on its stand. Karen didn't look happy, but then she likely wanted to reprimand Nina and couldn't. Right now, Sienna thought Karen was only her aunt. She didn't know Karen had been her CIA handler.

"What was that?"

Parker shifted to Sienna. "You should know. After all, you were planning to leave with her so she could protect you. She was making sure you'll be all right."

Karen gasped. "You absolutely cannot leave."

Sienna set her hands on her hips. "I'm not a prisoner. So far as I know. That means I can leave if I want to, which I hadn't actually decided on yet."

Karen shot her a look. "You've stayed alive all the time you've been here, haven't you? Why leave now?"

"Things have changed."

Sienna strode out of the kitchen. Parker waved off Karen and followed her out. He caught her at the bottom of the stairs, stalling her with his hand around her wrist. He could snap her bones if he gripped too tight. Sienna was delicate, but she was also strong.

She looked at his hand, then up at his face. "Aren't you leaving?"

"I do have to get back to work. There's pa-

perwork that needs to be done on the guy
we arrested."

She didn't say anything. Her eyes surveyed
his face, but aside from that she was completely still.

"Will you at least call me if you decide to
leave?" She had to know he cared about her.

"I'll put your number in my phone. Call me,
Sienna, so I have yours." Hopefully he didn't
sound desperate, but Parker wanted to be able
to contact her.

Her lips curled up in a small smile. "You
have to let me go now, Parker."

His fingers loosened, but he shook his head.
She had to know he wasn't going to just walk
away when she was in danger. There may not
be anything between them, given her memory
loss and the unanswered question of why she'd
never met him at the airport. But that didn't
mean he was willing to risk not being around
if she needed him.

Sienna knelt and pulled the shoebox from
under the bed. Outside, she heard Parker's
truck start and the engine rev as he drove away.

A cold settled in her stomach as she realized she was here without him. Some part of
her seemed to recognize him, as much as she
didn't want that to be the case. The last thing

she needed was a man she had no memory of expecting her to say a particular thing or act a particular way.

That kind of pressure—wondering if she was still the woman he'd known and who that was—would drive her crazy. Sienna felt crazed enough already. The CIA? It was enough to send her running out the door. With no memory, she was more than in over her head; she was drowning. Those men had tried to kidnap her, and she'd had no way to fight them off beyond the basic self-defense techniques she'd learned at the gym.

Sienna removed the rubber bands that secured the box and sat back on her heels. She flipped the lid onto the floor to reveal the contents.

A collection of photos with curled edges had been fastened with a rusty paper clip. The one on top was a country house and barn. Underneath the stack was an old movie ticket stub, two postcards from European cities that were blank on the back and enough space for the Bible Sienna had removed when she'd woken from her coma.

Nothing new. Nothing that made her remember what she was supposed to be doing. Or anything about who she was.

Did Nina really think Sienna hadn't looked

in the shoebox before? And what in here made Nina believe Sienna would leave her aunt?

The Bible had been a solace to her in the months she'd tried to get her memory back. Sienna had scoured its pages, reading and re-reading passages she had highlighted in her forgotten past. Notes she had made in the margins where it had spoken to her in one way or another. But none of that meant anything to her now—she had no frame of reference for it. She had read it as though for the very first time, soaked up the hope and peace found in those pages when so much of her life was up-side down.

Sienna flicked through the photos, but there wasn't anything tucked between them. She only saw images of people she didn't recognize in places she'd never been.

With a cry of frustration she dumped the shoebox over. She wanted to smash the thing, but then she'd have nowhere to store the secret treasures of a woman who didn't exist anymore. Maybe she never would.

On an exhale, Sienna righted the box and re-stowed the items. When it was secure, with the rubber bands replaced, she went to the closet and tucked it in her duffel. Who knew what the night would bring? If she had to run, she wanted the hidden things with her.

Sienna glanced at her closed bedroom door. Did she want to face her aunt? Karen was keeping secrets from her. Why else would she have asked Sienna if she had killed her attackers? Now Sienna knew why her aunt had thought that. But was it real? Was she a killer?

She got ready for bed. She was done with this awful day where her life had upended. With a sigh, she closed the bathroom door and went to the window. The night outside was dark, but the only light came from the living room to her right. Sienna had turned off her lamp so she could better see the stars, but it was cloudy. Not a night to dwell on the magnitude of things around her.

The backyard was an expanse of damp grass from the rains they'd had the past week, but was now twice as green. Bad with the good, just like everything in her life.

The trees swayed in the breeze, though her barn was silent. The animals were fine.

The quiet just reminded her that no one needed her. At least, not until she recalled whatever it was she'd forgotten. Then maybe everyone would stop giving her indecipherable looks or walking on eggshells as they bypassed her to get on with their important lives.

A flash of motion by the barn.

She'd painted it herself, because every barn

should be red. Plain wood was a travesty. Probably just a small animal foraging.

It moved again. Bigger than a critter. The size of a grown man.

FIVE

Parker swiped his card in the reader. The buzzer went off. He pushed open the heavy door and strode into the office. Despite it being way past midnight, at least half of those who worked there milled around. Their team and two others shared the floor, one of whom was in and prepping for an early-morning raid.

Wyatt sat behind his desk, peering intently at the screen on his computer.

Parker hung his coat on the back of his chair. "Did you lose your reading glasses again?"

Wyatt shot Parker a disgusted look that only made him laugh. They were all late thirties, and Wyatt bemoaned—constantly—the fact he'd been prescribed glasses for his headaches instead of less paperwork and more fieldwork.

Wyatt clicked his mouse. "Paperwork on the detainee is done. I put in a request for some background on him, but we likely won't know who he is until we run his prints. Even then, given his accent, we may be looking at Homeland Security or Interpol. Who knows where this guy surfaced from?"

Parker slumped into his chair. "My guess, they're going to show up as ex-military. Foreign, but the country won't matter much. One was Italian. The others weren't."

"So why is a team of foreign mercenaries trying to kidnap your girl-with-amnesia?" Wyatt grinned. "Is she some kind of spy?"

Parker stayed quiet.

"She is?" Wyatt busted up laughing. "Seriously? Little Sienna Cartwright is CIA?"

Parker was too tired; otherwise, he'd have thrown a paperweight at his partner. "I fail to see why this is funny. My guess, whatever her last mission was, it went unresolved and that's why she was almost abducted by foreign mercenaries."

Wyatt's smile dropped. "Whoa."

It had happened a few times. Those moments where it became clear there was a world between Parker's experience as a SEAL, traveling the world, meeting a CIA agent, and Wyatt's experience being a city police detective. Sure, they were both small-town US marshals, but the roads they had traveled to get there were vastly different.

Wyatt swallowed. "Jonah's on the phone

with the judge. Mr. Italiano can sit in holding tonight. In the morning we'll figure out who he is, and what's next for him."

Parker nodded. "Okay. Guess it's time to go get some sleep."

Wyatt waved off Parker's comment. "Sleep is for sissies."

Parker pulled his jacket back on and strode down the hall to find out from the duty marshal if their detainee had said anything. Any comment he made was a potential lead on whoever had targeted Sienna tonight. If they got something good, he'd be one step closer to walking away.

When he was sure she was protected, when she lost that shadow of fear in her eyes, then Parker's heart would finally be able to let her go.

He'd seen it in his dad, the desperation that wouldn't let him find peace after Parker's mom had run off with another man. He'd been eight at the time, and for the next ten years he'd watched his father drink away the pain of her betrayal.

History had repeated itself with his own ex-wife. Parker had prided himself on being stronger than the lure of the oblivion drinking would have given him. Instead, he'd thrown himself more and more into work—until he'd earned the nickname "Charger" because he wouldn't ever stop, no matter what was in front of him.

Most days he'd almost envied his dad the outlet of alcohol, the sting of betrayal had been that great. He'd thought he finally found what he'd wanted in Sienna. Then she'd betrayed him, as well.

Clearly, her work had been more important to her. Karen had told him as much, and he believed it. Despite the vulnerability in Sienna's eyes, and the sorrow when she'd told him she couldn't remember anything, it was clear she was just like every other woman—willing to do whatever it took to get what she wanted.

And it hadn't been him.

The duty marshal wasn't at his desk, and the door to the hall was open. Parker stepped through it, one hand on his weapon, into the commotion.

"...don't know! He asked for water..."

The open cell door was number four. A marshal stood over a man lying prone on the floor. The one from whose teeth Parker had pulled a capsule—a suicide pill. The duty marshal was on his knees by the man, arms stretched out, one palm over the other on the man's chest as he performed CPR.

The other marshal spoke into his phone.

"Yes, I need an ambulance." He rattled off their information so the EMTs and dispatched police officers would know what the situation was.

Parker knelt by the man and pressed two fingers to his neck. The duty marshal blew air into him and then listened to his chest.

"He's dead."

In the dark, tucked under her blankets, Sienna listened to the clock in her bathroom tick the minutes away. There hadn't been anyone outside. At least, not that she'd seen, and she'd waited a while to catch a glimpse of the person again.

Until she gave up believing she'd ever seen anyone.

But the nervous feeling remained, so much so that she just couldn't relax. If this went on much longer, she'd have to shut the bathroom door, instead of allowing that beam of light from the night-light in there to extinguish at least some of the pitch-black in her room. Just once in her life, Sienna would like to fall asleep without it taking hours.

Sienna shifted positions. She should be exhausted. Instead, her body—and her brain— were abuzz with everything that had happened.

The CIA.

Maybe she should get Nina's number from their caller ID and ask her what...

The window exploded. Glass shattered into the room as the rapid pop of gunfire sprayed across her bed and hit the wall to her right. Sienna rolled away from the window, taking the comforter with her, and slammed onto the floor. The noise was as loud as fireworks and shut out all other sound. Sienna clapped her hands on her ears and looked at her bedroom door. Bullets had splintered the wood, leaving dark holes all in a row across the door and the walls on either side. If there hadn't been a brick facade below the window outside, she would probably be dead.

Was it safe to try and get into the hall? Should she crawl under the bed?

More gunfire sprayed dust down around her as she huddled on the floor. Who was firing at her? What were they aiming at? This seemed more like spraying bullets, hoping they hit something. They weren't coming low enough to hit her, but her bed and the wall beyond had been obliterated.

Or maybe they didn't *want* to hit her. Just force her into a corner.

The gunfire stopped.

Sienna lifted her head. She didn't dare look over the bed. Completely still, she breathed in the dark and quiet, waiting to see if she would get shot the minute she tried to get out of her room.

Her cell phone was on the bedside table. Should she reach for it?

She shoved her limbs out of the tangle of her comforter, did a sit-up and reached for her phone.

Crack. Crack. Crack.

She fell back to the floor, phone in hand. *Thank You, Lord.* She really did not want to die. Where was Karen? Was she safe? Sienna breathed a prayer for her aunt. They may not be particularly close family, despite living together, but Sienna still cared if she was hurt. As she yelled, "Amen," against the deafening noise, she dialed Parker's number.

She hadn't figured she'd be using his number so soon. She hadn't even thought she would need it at all, if she was honest with herself. Why would she? He was useful in a pinch, but it wasn't like he could actually help get her memories back.

"Parker."

She barely heard him over the deafening noise. "It's Sienna." She had to yell. "Someone's shooting at me."

"I'll be there in five minutes. Stay wherever you are and do not move." His voice held a strand of authority that made her want to curl into herself and await his help. For now, she was willing to concede.

"I'll get police there, as well. Just sit tight."

"I am."

"That's good," he said. Like he cared, like it was important to him that she was okay.

The gunfire stopped.

"It's done. Again." Her voice sounded loud to her own ears.

"I still don't want you moving."

Sienna told him where she was. She hadn't had much in the way of support since she'd woken up from the coma. Aunt Karen wasn't the warm and caring type, and Sienna hadn't wanted to reach out not knowing how she truly felt about the woman.

Parker was like a beacon on a dark night.

Too bad she couldn't navigate in that direction. No matter how his voice, and his presence, tugged on her heart. No matter how capable he was. Because Sienna didn't know how she felt about him, either.

She started to army crawl toward the closet. What if she and Parker had argued? What if he'd wronged her and he didn't want to tell her now because it would cloud her judgment of him? What if she had wronged him?

As much as she wanted to believe she'd always been a good person, what did she really know? She might be a bad guy, one the CIA was keeping tabs on because she was some kind of enemy. They liked to keep those close, right?

She reached the walk-in closet and kicked the door shut. The flashlight on her phone was blinding. Sienna got dressed, then packed a couple of extra things in her already-full duffel. There was no way she was going to stay here, not when whoever had tried to abduct her had come to her home to try and kill her.

She pulled on her shoes.

A bang brought her head up. Then she heard his voice. "Sienna!" The light in her room flipped on.

"In the closet." She zipped up her jacket, still sitting on the floor. When Parker flung the door open, he had his gun in one hand. He held out the other and hauled her to her feet.

"You okay?"

She nodded and reached for her bag.

"You're dressed." His brow crinkled. "You weren't in bed? Are you going somewhere?"

"I was in bed. Now I'm leaving." She picked up her duffel and strode past him out of the closet. "They're closing in, first trying to kidnap me and now trying to kill me. I'm not waiting around for them to get the jump on me again like they did in the woods. No way. Not happening."

She really was not interested in dying before she got the answers to the puzzle in her head. Otherwise, she would never know what she'd forgotten—good or bad.

"You need to give the police your statement."

Sienna stopped at her bedroom door. There were so many bullets in it, it was a wonder the thing was still standing. She turned back to Parker, trying not to betray the way her insides shook. If she'd been right here minutes ago, she would be dead now. "Fine."

She wasn't going to obstruct justice. But as soon as she was done, she would be gone. That was why she ignored the look on his face and left him alone in her bedroom. Sienna had no emotional tie to this house, just the loss of a place she had considered safe. A bedroom she'd been able to rest in.

But no more.

She strode down the hall, trying to remember where she'd put the neighbor kid's number. She could pay him to care for the animals until she got set up somewhere else. He'd offered to help enough times.

The office door was open, her aunt on the phone perfectly healthy and not looking at all ruffled the way Sienna felt. Cops stood by the front door.

All thoughts of her livestock went out the window.

"Ms. Cartwright?"

She nodded. "That's me." Then tossed the duffel on the floor by her feet.

"Could you tell us what happened here?"

Parker watched Sienna speak with the officers. Men he knew. Men he trusted to find the person who'd shot at her tonight. Where did she think she was going to go? She had no memory of her skills for evasion, though she seemed to have the will to use them still. Why else would her first thought be to run?

Karen rolled to the office doorway.

"Did you check in with your people?"

She shot him a look. "We don't know who did this."

"And you're just going to lie to the police, say you don't know of any reason anyone would want to target Sienna?"

Karen rotated the chair toward him, a scowl on her face. "This is none of your business. Sienna Cartwright didn't want you in her life, not when you gave her the choice. And now she doesn't even know you. So don't think for one second she's going to fall over you in desperation for you to play the hero and solve all her problems. She's the only one who can get her memories back, and you trying to help won't achieve that. I've been waiting a year for her to remember."

"You were dead against us getting together from the beginning." She'd shown up at his house a few days after Sienna's no-show in Atlanta. Karen had insisted—as Sienna's handler—that he move on, but had he really?

"Why did you even let her move here?"

Karen rolled her eyes. "So I underestimated the connection. I thought she'd get over you, but some part of her brain was tied to this place." She glanced aside, up at him. "To you."

"But she doesn't remember me."

"She chose her work, you know that. She chose to continue her missions and not let emotion cloud her judgment. Right now you can't upset her recovery with all this wondering who you were to her. I need her focused on that last mission, on recovering the memories she forgot."

"The only way she can do that is by staying alive. I can help with both. You know I'll keep her safe." If he filled out the paperwork, Parker could get two weeks' vacation. Then he'd be able to focus on aiding Sienna in figuring all this out. The guy they'd arrested was dead, and they had no other outstanding cases that needed all of them. It was all little stuff. Nothing pressing. Almost like it had been designed that way, so he'd have the time to do this.

Years ago he'd have attributed that to God, but his faith had fallen by the wayside with everything that had happened. The personal betrayal by his wife and his friend. Sienna's turnabout, choosing her work after what he'd thought they had shared. The wars he'd fought, and the friends he'd lost. Now it was hard to see that God could be good, or that He loved Parker.

Karen didn't look all that happy to hand Sienna over to him.

"If I'm going to protect her, I'll need to know everything you know."

"I've put in the request. After I hear back is when I'll be able to share information."

Parker nearly rolled his eyes. "I can't know what's coming if you keep me in the dark."

At the end of the hall, Sienna shook hands with the officers and picked up her duffel. Parker pushed away from the wall and nodded to Karen. "If you'll excuse me."

The cops wanted to talk, but Parker just said, "Call me when you know something."

They needed to get out there and search for whoever shot at Sienna. But as with the men who'd tried to kidnap her, Parker didn't think the shooter's identity would give them anything. He needed to figure out who was hiring these people, and why they were doing this to Sienna.

Parker strode to the front door, determined to run after her. Where would she be going, anyway? Her truck was still broken down by the roadside, and he didn't think she'd leave Karen stranded. Was she going to hitchhike?

Parker strode onto the porch and clicked the locks on his truck, beside which were parked two cop cars. He was determined to find her wherever she might have run off to. But as he cracked open his door and the dome light came on, Sienna climbed in the passenger seat.

She looked so broken down. Not hurt physically. But for such a strong woman to have been brought low like this arrested him. Parker wanted to go to her and hug her until she felt better. But would she accept his comfort?

He shook away the thoughts and got in. "Where to?"

Sienna stared out the window. It was the second time tonight she'd been in his truck, and both times had been after she was almost hurt.

"How about some rest? You're probably exhausted, and my place is safe. I have a guest room."

She nodded, but didn't look over. He had a

million questions about what she wanted to do and where they should start, but he didn't have the heart to ask her. So he pulled out onto the road and glanced back at the porch. Karen was there, talking into a cell phone.

How long would it be before the CIA was on their tail? Parker had said his place was safe, but was that true? He couldn't know for sure he was making the right move.

He couldn't be sure if the CIA was even on their side.

SIX

Parker pulled into an apartment complex and turned right around the back of a row of three-story apartments. He reached over her to hit the garage door opener on her visor and then pulled inside.

Sienna stared. There was nothing in there. No tools, no freezer…nothing anyone might keep in their garage.

She opened her door wide enough so she could get out, but not so wide she'd hit the wall with the door of Parker's giant vehicle. Maybe his truck fit in here better, because this government vehicle certainly didn't.

"Something funny?"

She blinked up at him. When had he come up behind her? He took the opportunity to swipe her duffel from her hand. Sienna shook her head. The quicker they got out of this cramped space, the better. "Nothing. Lead the way."

She followed him into his kitchen. Half expecting empty pizza boxes and a sink full of dirty dishes, she was surprised to find only one plate and mug in there—probably from breakfast. Sienna pulled her attention from his kitchen so he didn't think she was stalking his nutritional choices.

The living room had one big leather couch and a chair that probably reclined to almost horizontal. His TV was gigantic, though he'd probably argue it was the right size for the room.

He dumped her bag by an open door to a bedroom and then passed her again going back into the kitchen. "Tea?"

She spun around. "Huh?"

He shook a box of the cinnamon tea she loved. "Want some?"

Sienna nodded, then slumped onto a vintage bar stool at the counter. She set her elbows on the surface and watched him fill a kettle.

"I'd have thought you'd be freaking out."

She ran her thumbnail along a split in the surface. "What makes you think I'm not?"

He glanced up, a conciliatory smile on his face.

"Maybe I just freak out quietly, instead of out loud." She glanced around. "Do you have paper and a pen?"

He pulled them from the end drawer and set them in front of her.

Sienna got the paper from her pocket. Sure, she had a shoebox of things that likely meant something to her once upon a time, but having been the only personal possession she'd had when she'd woken up, this verse had to mean something. Otherwise, why carry it on her?

Unfolding the sheet, she pressed it flat. She'd looked up the words, but couldn't find a match in her search. She'd figured it was a paraphrase she'd done to solidify the meaning by putting it in her own words.

Sienna picked up the pen. *Help me remember, Lord.*

She copied the words onto Parker's notepad. As she wrote, Parker rounded the counter to read aloud over her shoulder. "'Don't draw any conclusions when it's too early. God has to do that. He is the one who brings to light the hidden things. He's the one who reveals what each person has planned. He is the one who decides.'" He shook his head. "What does that mean?"

Sienna stared at it, not wanting to look at him when he was so close to her. She was already nervous enough. "I think I've forgotten something important." She blew out a breath. "Forgetting sounds so innocuous. I don't remember anything at all about myself or my life. But I think this means there was something important. I just can't pry it out of my head. This is a message—from me. To remind me to trust God's timing, instead of trying to force things."

"Is that going to work? I mean, until then, what? We just sit around doing nothing?"

Sienna shook her head. "We have to work at this, even while we're waiting." She hopped off the stool and went to her duffel. The shoebox was on top, so she set it on the counter and showed him what she had gathered. "As far as I know, it's a collection of memorable but otherwise insignificant stuff I've accumulated over the years."

Parker fingered the stack of photos. "Unless it isn't."

"What do you mean?"

"When I was on the phone with Nina, she said you hid something. These people who tried to take you tonight, they want whatever it is. They want you to tell them where it is."

Sienna shook her head. "Then why try to kill me in my bedroom?"

Parker's eyes were dark. "It's a pretty inept assassin who sprays a room with that many bullets and doesn't hit anything. Unless he's not actually trying to kill you."

Sienna had rolled off the bed. She'd gotten out of the way, and the shooter had continued to haphazardly spray the room. "Okay, so they were trying to scare me."

"Or jog your memory with a stressful experience."

She didn't like the idea of anyone attempting to force her to remember like that. "I *have* to remember. Kidnapping? Shooting at me? I can't afford to have amnesia anymore. This needs to be finished."

"What can you do? You can't just decide this is going to go away."

Sienna gritted her teeth. "I know that." Her voice was quiet, even to her own ears. "I just can't bear the thought of being helpless."

Parker set his hand on her shoulder. "You're not. I know you, Sienna. You're strong enough to beat this. The people threatening you, the memory loss. All of it."

She backed up so that his hand fell back to his side. "That's exactly the problem. You might know me, or so you say. But I don't know myself. I don't know what kind of person I was. I don't know what I had to learn or how to fight this. All I have is that shoebox and a piece of paper. Neither of which mean anything."

"You have me."

She shot him a look.

Parker's face twisted with something that looked almost like hurt. "I don't mean anything, either?"

"That's not it." She blew out a breath. "Up until six hours ago, I didn't even know who you were other than some random guy in town I'd have liked to talk to."

Yeah, so she'd been nursing a pretty terminal crush since the first days she and Karen had come here. The day she'd spotted him at the grocery store she'd been a goner. She'd been back there every week, same day, same time, hoping he'd be there, but it was two months before she saw him again.

He was a good-looking guy, no ring on his left hand. What was the harm in attraction? She'd needed something in her life that made her smile, even if they never talked to each other.

When he'd only acted weird with her, she had shut that down fast. Though apparently that was because he thought *she* was the one acting weird. How was she supposed to know they'd known each other?

She sucked in a breath. "Did I know you lived here?"

Parker's features softened. "I told you about this valley. You said…"

"What?"

"I'm not supposed to tell you anything, re-member? You're supposed to let it come back all by itself."

"Please." She grabbed his hand and squeezed. "Please tell me something."

He stared at her for a moment and then acquiesced. "You said you'd never really had a home. That Nina was your family. When I told you about my hometown, you said you'd love to see it. That you'd visit me when I was back."

Sienna shut her eyes. "She said she's my best friend."

"She's with the CIA, too. An operative."

Sienna was almost afraid to ask. "Do I…go on missions, as well? Like a spy?"

Parker nodded.

Sienna took two steps away, grabbed the hair on the sides of her face and tried to breathe. "I can't…I just… How?"

Parker wanted to hug her again. She was the strongest woman he'd ever met, and yet his re-action was to go to her with support. Why was that? It wasn't like there was much he could do to help her except tell her more.

"They recruited you and Nina out of col-lege. They had you finish your degrees—yours was international politics and Nina's was economics. You both had the same bad hair." He grinned. "Half the time you'd go to each other's classes and the professors couldn't tell the difference between you."

"We look alike?"

Parker nodded. "You said sometimes on missions you'd pretend to be the same person, and you'd use identical wigs. Anyone tracking you would see two people leave and never know which of you was the right woman to follow. Or you'd give each other an alibi when one of you was in public and the other was on a mission. You didn't get close to anyone." He shrugged. "People see…"

"What they want to see." Sienna looked up at him, her big brown eyes surrounded by all that blond hair. He could easily imagine her enchanting some unsuspecting target before he even realized he was being charmed out of sensitive information.

And two of them? The CIA must have thought they'd hit the jackpot with Nina and Sienna.

"That's crazy, but in a sort-of-cool way." She smiled for a second. "But doesn't that mean Nina should know what I did before I was in a coma? She has to know what I don't remember."

Parker shook his head. "She indicated you're

the only one with the knowledge of who these people are and what they want."

"How is that possible, when we worked so closely together?"

Parker lifted his hands and let them fall back to his sides. "If she calls, we can ask her."

Sienna perched on the back of the couch and hung her head. She'd really thought that paper from her pocket, and what was written on it, was going to solve this. He figured it was more likely that the answer was in the shoebox.

He crossed to it and looked through the things again. An old movie ticket, some photos. A few other things. Sienna wasn't the kind of person who kept souvenirs; CIA agents just couldn't do that. He pulled the paperclip from the photos and laid them on the counter of his breakfast bar. A little girl, blonde, maybe six years old, with an older boy, both completely covered with dirt, digging in a hole. Dirty smiles on their faces. A mountain. Two postcards. A ranch house with a red barn beside it.

Parker lifted the ranch picture and studied it. He felt Sienna come to stand beside him.

Her voice was quiet when she said, "Was that my house?"

He shook his head. "Not that you told me. Home was a mansion with your parents, then boarding school—where you met Nina—and later a condo on the beach in Virginia. You shared it with your friend, but you were never there at the same time. It was listed under one name, an alias both of you used."

He kept studying the picture. "If I had to guess, I'd say this was your uncle's ranch."

"Do you think this could be my brother? Do I have a brother?"

Parker didn't think she was ready for the answer to that.

He passed her the ranch picture. "This is why I said you only had an uncle. You told me he lived in northern California on a cattle ranch. You loved to go there when you were a little kid."

Sienna blew out a breath and wound up yawning. She was fading fast.

"Look, it's really late. Why don't you sleep on all this? We can figure out a plan in the morning of what to do next."

Relief flooded her face as she nodded. "If I can sleep."

"I'll be in the next room if you need anything. Just holler or bang on the wall."

A smile curled her lips. Parker pulled her to him and gave her a loose hug. "Sleep well, okay. We'll figure this out."

She nodded against his chest. "Thank you."

She trailed to the guest room and hauled up

her duffel on the way past. When she shut the door, Parker exhaled. He'd gotten accustomed to the emptiness of his apartment, but it almost felt right having her here. Too bad he couldn't get used to it, or she'd leave an even bigger hole when she left this time.

He hoped the shoebox of things, and what was locked in Sienna's memory, was the clue they needed to find whatever was out there.

Parker pulled out his phone and took a picture of the ranch house. He sent the information he knew to one of the forensic guys at the office and asked him to get an address. It wouldn't be fast—it could even be days—but Parker would take whatever he could get.

The picture of Sienna and the little boy was gone. She must have taken it into the bedroom with her. Parker's heart clenched. He couldn't imagine how she felt, wondering if there was someone she was supposed to be missing, someone she was supposed to love, but who she couldn't remember at all.

He glanced at the photos on his dresser. His collection—like he figured was true of Sienna's—represented the pieces of his past he wanted to carry with him. His first SEAL team, all in a huddle, sweaty after a rough-and-tumble football game in some desert country. Playing pool on a ship. Going for a run in Alaska in their shorts for the fun of it.

Those men were his family. Older guys retired, like Parker had, when they found themselves slowing down. It was necessary to put the mission first for the last time in their careers. Others had been killed or injured. A few lived close enough that he hung out with them sometimes. Every picture held meaning.

He thumbed his phone, but there were no new texts or calls. Didn't Nina want to give him her number in case he needed to call her? Evidently that was a one-way street. But he did have Karen's number and the landline at Sienna's house. He'd looked that up at work.

Parker sat on the edge of his bed and dialed. He just couldn't rest until he knew more. Despite what he'd told Sienna about waiting until the morning, he needed a plan before he could sleep.

Karen's voice was groggy when she picked up the phone. "Yes?"

"It's Parker."

Rustling. "Is she okay?"

"She's sleeping."

"Then what do you want?"

He didn't care for her attitude. He was determined to get what he needed to help Sienna. "I want to know what her last mission was."

"That's classified."

"What do you need that she doesn't remember?"

"Also classified."

Parker fisted his free hand on his knee. "Do you want them to torture it out of her?"

"Of course not."

"Then tell me what I'm looking for. What is it they want?"

Karen sighed. "A PIN-coded flash drive."

"And Sienna knows where it is, somewhere in her memory?"

"Yes. Before she nearly died, she hid the flash drive. We have no idea where. There was a time crunch, and she didn't have time to call in. We need that flash drive back. It *cannot* fall into the wrong hands. That outcome is unacceptable. This is highly sensitive information." Karen paused, breathing hard. "*Highly* sensitive."

"Okay. Get the flash drive, don't give it to anyone else. Got it."

"And if she doesn't remember?"

Parker shrugged, even though she couldn't see it. "I'll keep her safe from them until she does." He paused. "I take it these are big players."

"The biggest."

He had to know his enemy in order to out-think them. "And you're going to send me everything you have on them?"

"Not on your life."

"So I'm supposed to do this blind?"

"I'm sure you can handle it."

Parker was sure he could deal with armed assailants. It was the handling of Sienna that he was worried about. Her memories could come back in pieces, or all in one go or not at all. They couldn't control it, or predict what would happen. No amount of pressure would help her remember.

"Oh, and one more thing."

"What's that?" Karen couldn't think that he was going to give her much of anything if she wasn't prepared to give him even basic information.

"As soon as she contacts you I want a location on Nina Holmes. She needs to be brought in."

SEVEN

Sienna's night had provided little rest. She'd tossed and turned as she remembered gunshots shattering the windows of her bedroom. Thankfully, she had managed to get a couple of hours of sleep.

Now they were on the road again, and she was glad Parker had waited until they were in the car before he laid out the details of his conversation with Karen. At least she was sitting down when he'd told her the news—though she'd rather he'd let her be somewhere she could pace. She needed room to move.

Nina was wanted by the CIA.

Parker laid his hand on hers as if sensing she needed his support. Her other hand gripped the door handle.

She quickly let go of both and fisted her hands on her thighs. "Does that mean Nina is helping us, or is she working for whoever is after me?"

Was she wrong about her supposed friend? If Sienna couldn't trust her gut, then what— or who—could she trust? Even sitting with Parker in his SUV, she still felt completely alone. He was little more than a stranger, but she thought that she could believe in him. How could she be sure?

Parker shrugged as he drove. "I guess we'll find out where Nina's allegiances lie one way or the other."

"And you managed to get an address on my uncle's ranch? Did you sleep at all?"

"A little." Now it was after six in the morning and they were in the car by consensus. Who wanted to hang around when she could be getting her memories back?

She didn't know whether to get her hopes up that the ranch would provide answers. They were headed there now, hoping it would jog something in her mind. If she cared enough about the ranch to have kept a picture of it, then maybe she'd felt it was secure enough to hide a flash drive there.

Sienna couldn't believe her life was in danger over something as small and innocuous as a flash drive. Though whatever information was on it likely wasn't harmless. Why else would the CIA want it back so badly? Why

would one person try to kidnap her, and someone else shoot up her bedroom?

Lord, help us find it.

She had no problem handing it over to Karen
if that would stop the threats against her. This
whole situation was some kind of crazy multi-
pronged attack. If they were working with one
another or instead competing for the flash
drive, then she needed to watch her back, her
front and both sides.

Sienna pulled her cell phone from her purse
and sent Karen a text.

You're not my aunt, are you?

Within seconds the reply came. I'm your
handler.

"Everyone's been lying to me. Karen, making me think she was my aunt. Nina, lying by
not telling me I have a best friend. Allowing
me to believe there was no one who cared."
She shot Parker a look. "You."

"What about me?" His jaw was set.

"You tell *me*. I obviously should've known
who you were. I picked this place to live, thinking I had some kind of tie to this town. Am I
not supposed to conclude that tie was you?"

Parker lifted his hot cup and took a sip. Trying to decide what to tell her?

Sienna glanced toward the window. "If you're going to lie or tell me a half-truth, then don't bother saying anything. I don't want to hear it."

The highway went south, through farms and tiny towns into northern California. The landscape was all green, trees and fields. Mountains peaked with snow. Beautiful country, but unfamiliar. Like everything else in her life.

The only thing which resonated with her even vaguely was when she read her Bible. The solace in those pages gave her peace, but she struggled to draw on that now. Did she have enough faith that it would survive this trial? She could only pray she did.

"If I tell you, how will you know it's the truth? And what's the point, anyway? It isn't like we can go back to that place. I thought we had something and you chose your job instead. That was it. I care about you, but rehashing everything that went down between us doesn't mean anything when you walked away from it."

He sounded so dejected Sienna glanced at him. She had chosen her job over him? And what did he mean they'd had something? Were they more than the friends he'd insinuated they'd been? She could see falling for someone like him. Tall, strong. The all-American hero she'd initially seen. That hadn't let up, given he'd been there when she needed him and even brought her to his house. Taken vacation days just to help her.

By his own admission he cared. And Sienna knew she cared about him. She hadn't felt this safe in months. Maybe not even since she woke up. It had been incredibly disorienting, not knowing who she was or who these people were who'd expected her to remember them.

Would she ever remember him?

"Though evidently I was memorable enough that you told Nina all about me."

"She's my best friend, of course I told her." When Parker shot her a look, Sienna said, "I don't have to remember her to know that. It's a sacred girl code."

Parker huffed. "I don't know about girl codes. I was a SEAL. You don't get much more not-girlie than that."

"I can imagine." She glanced at him. Should she ask? "Is…that how we met?"

After a moment of quiet, he finally nodded. "We were sent in to rescue you and an asset you were with. Brought you back to safety, then went back and finished the mission."

"All-American hero."

Parker looked over. "Huh?"

Sienna shook her head. "Nothing important."

Parker was the kind of man who knew how to separate his feelings from the job, and that was what he was doing now. He couldn't know that she was growing attached to him, even if it was only because he'd been there for her. He wanted to help, and she was letting him. So what if that meant she just didn't want to be alone?

Parker had to keep thinking it was true that she'd wanted her job more than whatever relationship they'd had. She didn't want him to worry she liked him. Though what wasn't there to like? For whatever reason she'd cut things off between them, Sienna had to stick with that. At least until she knew for sure either way.

Parker changed lanes without indicating. His brow had furrowed as he studied the rearview.

"Is there something wrong?"

His jaw worked side to side. "There might be someone following us."

Sienna wanted to turn and look out the back window. The glass was tinted, but if there was someone back there, she didn't want to be the one who gave away the fact that they were on to them.

"What are you going to do?"

The highway was headed south. It wasn't difficult to predict where they were going when the road only went one direction. But were they only being tailed, or was their pursuer planning something?

Parker glanced at the signs for the next exit.

"Are we getting off the highway?" All that was there were two fast-food places and a gas station with a car wash.

He sped up. After they passed the exit, Parker cut right and sailed down the lane at the last minute. Sienna glanced back then. A compact car cut across two lanes in front of a semi and followed them.

"You didn't lose them."

"I know." Parker's jaw flexed. "But now we know for sure they're actually following us."

"So what now?" He'd pulled into the gas station parking lot, but their tank was still almost full. They'd refueled not too long ago. "What are we going to do? Shouldn't we be trying to get rid of our tail?"

He headed across the lot. "We're going to get the car washed."

Parker grabbed his debit card and the receipt from the machine, then pulled the SUV into the car wash. "Any idea who it is?"

Sienna glanced back.

"Middle-aged white male, brown cap. Dark jacket. Can't see any distinguishing features."

She turned so their eyes met. "Is that what you meant?"

Parker nodded. If they'd had more time, he might have touched her cheek. He might have tried to find the words to tell her how amazing he thought she was, facing all this with no memory. No recall of the skilled woman she used to be.

He looked away, out the back window. The man following them pulled out of the line for the car wash. If it was Parker, he'd be driving around to the front to await their exit and make his attack on them before they knew what was happening. But it was his job to stop the man from doing exactly that—and to keep Sienna safe in the automatic car wash while he did.

He slipped the vehicle into Neutral, leaned over and flipped the latch on the glove box. The weapon inside was unloaded. He handed it to Sienna and then passed her the magazine.

"Slide it up hard. Pull back…"

Sienna cocked it.

"The safety…"

She flipped the safety off.

"Okay, then." Parker couldn't see the man behind them.

"I didn't like feeling unsafe. I took a class and learned how."

He grabbed the door handle by his side.

"Stay here. If your life is at risk, you fire at your attacker and you aim to kill. There is no other reason to shoot a gun at someone. But you do not leave this car. That weapon is only for an emergency, and it is the farthest thing from what I want to happen to you. I'll be back in a few minutes. You only need to sit tight."

Thankfully, she nodded with no argument.

Parker breathed a sigh of relief and hopped out of the car. He ducked between the swirling brushes and got sprayed in the face as he sprinted to the entrance. With his shoulder against the wall, he checked the area outside. When he was sure it was clear, he raced out, weapon out in front and angled down, two hands on the grip. He circled the outside of the car wash.

Months ago, Sienna would have been right beside him step for step. Just as capable as he was at going up against this assailant. While part of him mourned the loss of the connection they'd had, he was also glad for the opportunity to protect the woman she was now. Not that the helpless female should be grateful the big strong man could keep her safe. Even when there was nothing between them, not a trace of the fact that he might've traded everything he'd had for her, he still wanted to be the one she turned to.

He might even go so far as to thank the God that Sienna prayed to for the chance to be the one who kept her safe when she needed it the most.

He glanced around the corner of the building. The sight of the car that had followed them, now angled toward the exit where Sienna would emerge, snapped him out of his thoughts. A man stood between the body of the car and the open driver's door. His weapon wasn't visible, but Parker wouldn't take for granted what he couldn't see. No one came to a fight without first arming themselves. Not if they expected to live through it.

Parker ducked between two cars parked by the gas station's small store and pulled out his phone. He only had seconds before the SUV, and Sienna, emerged from the car wash. Phone first, he lifted up, zoomed in and then snatched a picture of the man as best he could from this distance and angle. He would be able to email it in to the office later that morning. Then hopefully they'd be able to get an identity on this man.

His wet clothes were plastered to his body, chilling him in the early-morning air. Parker got close enough so that he saw the man reach into the back of his waistband below his jacket and draw something out.

"Drop it and put your hands on your head." He used his best "cop" voice.

The man spun. He was older, middle-aged, which to Parker's late thirties meant the man was pushing sixty. The man's eyes narrowed and he started to draw his weapon up.

Parker didn't move except to widen his stance. "Don't."

The front end of the car was all the way out. Sienna had climbed into the driver's seat. She glanced around and spotted him.

"Put it down." He didn't want to shoot this guy, whoever he was. But neither could he let the man continue to follow them every step of the way on their search for the flash drive.

The SUV's engine revved.

The man flinched but didn't turn to see what was behind him. And he didn't drop his gun or run away.

Sienna drove toward them. She picked up speed as she got closer and closer to the car and the man. Parker started to back up.

The SUV slammed into the back left corner of the car. The engine revved again as she used the size and momentum of Parker's vehicle to ram the car. Metal crunched against metal as Sienna pushed the car sideways.

The man yelped and dove out of the way. Parker ran around the car to the SUV. She stopped. The gunman was up. Parker flung the rear door open as shots hit the window on the opposite side. Glass shattered and Sienna screamed.

"Drive!"

The SUV shot away and sideswiped the car once more. Gunshots slammed into the back quarter panel and back window as they bumped the curb out of the gas station.

Parker's phone rang. He pulled it from his pocket as he climbed into the front passenger seat.

He offered a distracted "Yes?" and swiped most of the glass from the seat with his sleeve.

"It's Nina."

"You have interesting timing."

Karen had indicated Nina wasn't to be trusted. Unless it was some kind of personal difference that put them at odds, there had to be a reason for it. There was no way of knowing, given he or Sienna couldn't exactly pick up the phone and call the CIA and ask.

It could just be that Karen simply didn't want Nina to hinder Sienna's search. Nina had proven to be helpful so far, and he wasn't going to completely shut her out.

He glanced at Sienna; her eyes were wide as she gripped the steering wheel. Had the adrenaline of the past few minutes jogged loose any memories? He couldn't be sure until they got some downtime and he could ask her. "Are you on that guy behind us? Is that why you're calling?"

He glanced over his shoulder but couldn't see out the cracked back window.

"What guy? I'm working a different angle. What happened? Is Sienna okay?"

"Just a stray following us. She's shaken up, but other than that I think she's fine." Beside him Sienna nodded. "She's fine."

"Good." Nina sounded relieved.

Parker smiled as he looked toward the side window. This woman wasn't going to give him any slack if Sienna got the slightest scratch. He would get the full force of her ire in return for any harm that came to her friend.

That kind of love was hard to find. Though Parker had looked plenty—and even thought he'd had it for himself a couple of times. The fact that Sienna had it with her friend was a very good thing, and he was happy for them both even if maybe a little jealous.

If he and Sienna ever got to the place where they could try again to find a relationship, would he be brought into their fold? He couldn't see how it would happen immediately, but maybe after a time he would feel like part of their makeshift family.

Parker shoved aside the train of thought and said, "What did you need?" He would support Nina's effort as much as he could.

"Karen doesn't want me to interfere, but I sent her on a tangent. I want to meet up with you guys. Where are you headed?"

Parker explained about Sienna's uncle's ranch.

"That's the best idea I've heard in a year."

Parker had another one. "Can I send you the picture I took of the man following us?"

"Definitely."

If she could get an identity for them, it would put them a step closer to figuring out the mission Sienna had been on and what was on that flash drive everyone wanted.

Parker hung up and went in his phone gallery for the one he'd taken of the man. Sienna jerked the steering wheel hard to the right and pulled over. She put the SUV in Park with the front right wheel on the sidewalk. When Parker looked up her attention was on the phone.

Before he could ask, she said, "I know who that is."

EIGHT

"Wait a second." Sienna frowned. "Let me gather my thoughts. You look mad. Did I not do the right thing, hitting his car with yours? I was acting on instinct. Was that okay?"

She couldn't see that too much damage had been done to Parker's car. The man who'd been following them, on the other hand, his car was crumpled all down one side. She was pretty sure she'd popped one tire. He wouldn't catch up to them anytime soon.

Parker shifted the phone in his hand. She knew he wanted to talk about the photo, but she had to get past this moment first. The memory was still piecing itself together in her head, and she needed more time.

The adrenaline of the moment rushed through her. It fired synapses and made her feet jittery. She tapped the steering wheel even though they were still parked on the side of the road in the middle of the day. Someone driving past would think they were up to something or in trouble.

"Sienna."

She glanced at him.

"There's no reason to second-guess yourself. Don't worry about the truck—it's not a problem. Trust what you learned with the CIA, even though you don't remember it. It's like muscle memory. Buried in there is everything you need to keep yourself safe."

She hadn't even thought of that. Could she really have all those spy skills she saw in movies? Escape and evade tactics, or whatever they were called. Did Sienna have those, buried somewhere in her brain? And why didn't he act like that was a good thing? Parker was upset about something, or his mouth wouldn't be pinched like that.

His gaze was like a laser that pinned her to the driver's seat. "You did what you thought was necessary to save my life, right?"

Sienna nodded. Her only thought had been to keep that man from shooting him. Parker was obviously trained, but tell her nervous heart that in the moment. She'd only been thinking he couldn't get hurt. That she wasn't going to allow it.

"Go with that."

He knew. Sienna looked away, because he knew exactly why she had hit the other man's car.

The warmth of his fingers touched her chin. Sienna let him turn her head until she saw a matching warmth in his eyes. Had anyone ever looked at her like that before? "Parker." His name was a whisper from her lips.

His face filled her vision as he shifted in his seat. His lips drew closer to hers until they were only a hairbreadth apart. Why did this seem so familiar? So comforting? Like everything she had ever wanted, and the only place she wanted to be. The peace of being wanted— needed. The comfort of strong arms.

And for some reason…she'd given it up.

"Why did I walk away?"

Parker sucked in a breath and backed off.

"I want to know."

He was pulling away, and she was going to lose this connection—the chance to find out what she'd done to them. Why on earth would she have given him up? "I want to know why I chose to leave."

He stared out the front window. "You chose not to come." All warmth had evaporated out of his voice, leaving only a lack of emotion she didn't like at all. Why was he doing that?

Parker sighed. "We were supposed to meet

up at the airport in Atlanta. We'd talked about nothing else for days, and when the time came…you never showed. You left me standing there, alone, for four hours, waiting for you to show up."

She'd hurt him.

"I'm sorry."

He speared her with his gaze. "For what?"

She didn't know why she hadn't been there, but she could still be sorry for the pain she'd caused him. Was she so heartless that he wouldn't accept an apology for the obvious way she'd blown him off? No. If anything, Sienna thought she might have too much emotion.

Either she didn't know how to divorce her circumstances from her heart and how to compartmentalize the mission and her personal life, or Parker was the one person in the world who blew through her defenses and left her wide open. It was like he'd flooded every part of her since he pulled up behind her in his truck.

She had to know which.

Sienna prayed for courage to accept the answer, whatever it was. "So I just…never showed, and then nothing? I didn't give you any kind of explanation?"

"It wasn't that you'd been hurt. Whatever put

you in a coma came later. I know that much."
Parker paused. "You did send me a message."

"I did?"

"Karen showed up at my apartment two days later."

Sienna studied his face, but he wasn't giving away anything.

"She said you chose the mission—your work—over us."

Sienna shook her head. "Why would I do that?"

Parker's eyebrows lifted. "You just did."

"That makes no sense." She could hardly believe she'd chosen whatever there was at work over this man beside her. Karen had to have the answer. Sienna would get to the bottom of it just as soon as this was over.

"It doesn't matter now, it's done." Parker's heart didn't agree, but he wasn't going to let Sienna know that.

Just as soon as she remembered why she hadn't shown up, she would be leaving again. If he let her back in his heart now, he'd only have to try and dig her out when she walked away. Again. It had been painful enough the first time; he didn't know if he could handle another.

He was weak.

For all his physical strength, on the inside Parker was just like his dad. He was going to spend the rest of his life pining for a woman who didn't want him. Not that he had any intention of drowning his sorrows in a bottle. So far he'd made sure he never even got into a position where he might fall into drinking just to try and numb the pain. But that only meant he was left with that aching, gnawing wound Sienna had inflicted.

He unlocked his phone so the photo was on-screen again. "Just tell me about this. You said you knew who this was."

He had to get something from her, and at this point the job was all there was between them. Her last mission. Her memories. Her answers.

And when it was done, he was going to be the one who walked away.

He would have to. It was the only way Parker was going to survive. Enough of all this unspoken back-and-forth between them. They were nothing but acquaintances with a past she didn't even remember. He should take a page out of her book and choose his life—and his sanity—over her. Thank you, and goodbye.

Sienna studied the picture. He tried not to let the vulnerability he saw on her face penetrate, but it was tough. He had to steel himself against all that she was. Every single part of her beckoned to him like a lighthouse. But lighthouses were meant to keep people away from disaster. And that was what Sienna was to him. She was the potential for a disaster he was never going to recover from.

Parker lifted the phone. "Who is this?"

Her lips moved, her voice a whisper. "Thomas Loughton."

Sienna clapped her hand over her mouth. "You remember him?"

She frowned. "I don't know. I have his name, those two words in my head. Other than that, nothing. I couldn't tell you the first thing about who he is, or why he might be following us." She shook her head. "How did I know that? I don't know you. I don't know Nina. How do I know this guy?"

Parker shrugged like it was no big deal, though it stung to hear her say she didn't know him. While he could bring to mind every single word they'd ever said to each other, she didn't remember him at all.

He blew out a breath and let go of his spiraling thoughts. He opened his browser and did a basic internet search for Thomas Loughton. The results made his eyebrows lift.

"Newspaper article. 'Former NSA analyst Thomas Loughton was recently fired under suspicion of espionage. He was questioned by an internal review board, but no formal charges were brought. Disgraced, Loughton returned to his childhood home in Connecticut but hasn't been available for interview since."' Parker glanced up at Sienna. "That was eighteen months ago."

Her eyes were wide. "The NSA?"

"That's what it says. Which begs the question why a former NSA analyst suspected of what I would guess is leaking sensitive information is following us."

"Me."

"What?"

It was like she was trying the idea on for size, getting a feel for processing the details in her brain in the hope it would jog more memories loose. "He's following me." Sienna glanced out the front window. "The NSA. Thomas Loughton."

Sienna could see the question; it was on his face. But there was so much swirling in her head, what was she supposed to think? She'd remembered something! Sure, it was only one name, but Sienna wasn't going to miss the opportunity to celebrate this victory.

The fact that she didn't remember anything else was frustrating to say the least. It wasn't like that one memory had opened the flood-gates and everything came rushing back. Unfortunately. She knew God wouldn't just hand over everything she wanted right there in the moment. Often there was something to learn that she never would have grasped if He simply gave her what she asked for.

Parker fiddled with his phone again.

"Should I keep driving?"

"One second. I want to make another call." Parker held the phone out and it rang on speaker so she could hear it, too. Sienna shot him a grateful smile. He stared at her mouth for a second.

"Hello?"

Parker blinked. "Yep."

"What?" The voice through the phone was Nina.

"Nina, it's Sienna." She frowned at him. "And Parker." Was he losing his mind?

Parker shook his head. "We're here. We have a question for you."

"Shoot."

Sienna's lips curled up. Her friend was a hoot, but she was glad Parker was taking the lead on this. She was exhausted and hungry. She looked at the dash. It was way past lunchtime.

"Do you know if any of this has to do with former NSA analyst Thomas Loughton?"

Nina gasped. "She remembered?"

"Only his name." Sienna couldn't get too excited about that. "Nothing else."

"That's good. That's really good." Nina let out a frustrated groan. "But Thomas Loughton? If he's the seller, then this is worse than I thought."

"What do you know about him?" Parker asked.

"Not much more than office rumblings. Loughton, during his tenure with the National Security Agency, downloaded their encryption algorithm on to a flash drive. It's the key that lets you into their computer system. Anyone with a log-in ID and password and that flash drive can hack the NSA from anywhere in the world. It would only work for a short time before they caught on, but you could still do serious damage in that brief period. And if you were smart, you could move locations and send everyone on a wild-goose chase while you brought them down from the inside. Every agent and every asset we have in every country would be in danger."

"And Loughton stole it?"

"Yes," Nina said. "Most figured Loughton's intention was to give up everyone in covert operations by selling the flash drive to the highest bidder and then retiring to some non-extradition-treaty country and living the high life in paradise. This thing puts all of us—our identities and our missions—in jeopardy. It puts our secrets in the hands of the bad guy with the most money. I only figured it was a rumor. I never believed it was based on truth, since no one ever found any evidence he'd really done it."

Parker said, "But if it's true, then…"

"The NSA and the CIA must have covered it up because they knew everyone would go crazy trying to get their hands on it."

"What was Sienna's part in this?"

"We always gave each other all the details of our missions, in case one of us was ever compromised. Or burned." Nina was silent for a moment. "Except this one. But she must have been tasked with getting it back."

Sienna didn't know if she even wanted to remember what had happened to her. "Loughton is on our tail now, so he must be trying to get his hands on the flash drive."

"We still don't know who the buyer was going to be," Nina said. "But I think Thomas Loughton must have been biding his time, waiting for you to remember where you hid it, so he can get it from you and sell it for real this time. He must still want his retirement money."

Beside her, Parker shook his head. Did he wish he'd killed the man in the gas station? If he had, this would be over. Thomas Loughton would be dead and no longer a threat to them. But neither would they have any answers, the buyer's identity or the truth about what had happened.

His mouth worked back and forth, and then he said, "The ranch is still our best chance at finding the flash drive."

"I can meet you there," Nina said. "Give you some backup in case Thomas shows."

Sienna nodded. "That would be good." More because she would get to see her friend than because they needed help. Maybe seeing Nina would loosen more memories.

Parker set a plan with Nina and then ended the call.

Sienna started the engine. "I want to finish this mission." Parker turned to her, but she kept talking. "It's the only way I'm ever going to re-member, and the only way I'll be able to move on from this. I want my life back."

With the bad memories would come the good—and the answers about what had happened between her and Parker. She wanted to know so that she could make her choice about him again. Whether that meant she fell for him in a forever way or if it meant she walked away for the second time, Sienna didn't know.

But she wanted the chance to find out.

NINE

They were less than thirty miles from the ranch, and Parker was driving.

"Understood," he said into the phone. "Thank you for your time." He hung up from his call with the local county sheriff and said to Sienna, "We're clear to go to the ranch. No one should bother us."

She'd remembered Thomas Loughton's name. Was this trip to her uncle's ranch, a place she'd visited as a child, going to jog yet more memories? He hoped so.

"So what's the plan when we get there?" she asked.

Parker knew she was desperate to know who she was. But it couldn't be denied that some things might be best left forgotten.

"Loughton will find a way to catch up. We need to be cautious now we know who is on our tail and why. We can't underestimate what he's willing to do to get that flash drive."

She shifted in her seat. "Do you think he's the one who shot up my bedroom?"

Parker nodded. "Maybe he was even just trying to force you to leave the house to try and find the flash drive."

"Doesn't that mean we're doing exactly what he wanted us to do, then—find the flash drive? If I'd just stayed home, there would be no reason for him to come after me."

"But he would. He'd keep coming and coming, because Loughton's not going to stop until he gets his hands on what's his."

Parker had met plenty of guys like him. Men—and women, he guessed—who thought nothing of hurting people in order to succeed. That was why he had to protect her, because Sienna didn't know what she was getting into. They couldn't afford to underestimate Loughton.

He said, "We're not playing into his hands. You're the one in charge here. No one gets what they want until you find that flash drive. The person with all the answers here is you."

"But I don't remember."

"You're starting to." Parker glanced at her. "Trust your head to release the past when you're ready for it." He was talking as much about her last mission as he was about their relationship. "Your mind knows how important this is. It's locked up your memories of this experience, along with everything else, for a reason. But your brain got as much training as your muscles. When it's ready, it will turn the key a little more, and a little more and the past will come back to you."

"Please, Lord." Her entreaty was a whisper.

He knew she had faith in God, but a Heavenly Father wasn't something Parker was that interested in. Still, he could admit to being curious that the faith Sienna had possessed before she lost her memories was still part of her even now. Had Karen encouraged it? He did see a peace in Sienna that seemed to fly in the face of what was going on.

When this was all over, he'd have to ask her about why that was.

When the GPS instructed him to make a right turn down a dirt lane, Parker did so. The ground was rutted and sent the SUV up on the left side and then down, over and over. Finally the main house, a run-down prefab structure, came into view.

He watched Sienna's face for signs of recognition as she surveyed the area.

"Who owns this property?"

He parked and turned to her. The sun was beginning its climb down the sky, and while they'd stopped for dinner, neither had eaten overly much. Sienna was probably as eager as he was to stretch her legs.

"Let's walk while we talk." Maybe then they'd find a place to start searching on these acres of land for one tiny flash drive. It almost made Parker want to pray about the outcome.

Sienna strode to the front of the SUV where he stood. Together they turned to the expanse of land. Rolling hills and trees that disguised the entrance to a network of caves Sienna had told him she'd played in as a child.

They began to walk across the field. "It belonged to your uncle—you already know that. He passed away a little over four years ago, and after that, ownership transferred to your father."

Sienna glanced over. "Do I like him?"

Parker hesitated. It was an interesting question, one that spoke of the things buried in her mind. All of it wrapped up with the little boy in the photo. "You haven't spoken to your parents in years, and the last you told me was that you have no intention of ever contacting them."

"Why?"

Parker stopped. "Do you want to hear it, even if it's difficult? Even if the thing you don't know is tragic?"

Sienna swallowed. "I need to know it all. It's part of me."

"You're not missing anything if you never find out. You're still you."

"But I'll never know that for sure."

Parker studied her face. "When you were eight, your brother—he was older than you by five years—he drowned." He set his hands on her shoulders. "He was your best friend and your favorite person in the world. After he died, your parents went cold. That's how you described it. They sent you to boarding school. You said that it was to keep from losing you, too. But they did, anyway. It was there at school that…"

"God gave me Nina."

Parker nodded. For the first time since she'd shown up in his town, she was most like the woman he remembered. Those were the exact words she'd given him the first time. *God gave me Nina.*

Her brother had drowned? Sienna couldn't imagine how painful that had been to experience.

But she didn't remember it.

Parker angled left. "Let's head…"

She pointed. "That way." She'd already seen the cave entrance in the rolling hills overlooking the ranch house and barn and two other smaller outbuildings. The doors hung from broken hinges and a lot of the windows were broken. The whole place was so forlorn.

Underground seemed the most obvious place to hide something where it would lay unaffected by weather, animals or people looking for stuff to steal from an abandoned house.

Her father had really let the ranch become this? She could easily imagine it as a beautiful place with fields of crops and animals grazing. Washing hung out on a line. The scent of fresh-baked bread wafting through the kitchen window as she ran past, her brother right behind her.

"Come on, Sienna."

She pumped her arms and legs to catch him, but he was so fast. They crossed the field and Tim disappeared into the cave. "Come on, Sienna."

His voice echoed through the hollow ground and bounced off the dirt-packed walls. Jagged stone pricked her palm as Sienna traced her way down the tunnel to the open room. Her flashlight cast an eerie yellow glow that failed to dispel the dark.

Where was Tim?

Sienna sucked in a breath. "His name was Tim."

Parker's arm was around her. All she could

hear was her own breath, loud in her ears as she panted into the darkness.

She shook her head, trying to rid herself of the frightening memory. "I don't think I would have come here. But then, maybe that means it's exactly where I did come." She tried to think, to know what she couldn't know because she didn't remember.

"I don't know what to do. I have no idea where I hid the flash drive. This is pointless." She groaned and kicked at the dirt.

Parker stood silent and steady beside her, waiting. For what, she didn't know. Who knew when she was going to remember? He wasn't going to wait around forever. His vacation would only last so long, and then Parker would have to go back to his life as a marshal.

Sienna would be left with…not much. Unless she could remember.

A step. Another. Sienna moved farther into the darkness, Parker right there with her. She wouldn't find her brother this time, but maybe she would find the flash drive.

The tunnel opened and she found herself looking at the room she'd just pictured in her mind, the room where her brother had hidden. She took the flashlight from Parker and scanned until she found the tiny space, barely big enough for a child to crawl into. She'd circled the edge that day, and Tim had stayed silent until Sienna came close to him.

He'd reached out and grabbed her ankle, and Sienna had screamed while her brother erupted into laughter. The noise had been deafening in the small space. Her uncle had come running, thinking something terrible was happening. That had only made her brother laugh more.

It was one of the few times her uncle had smiled, seeing Sienna get all mad and kick her brother. The man hadn't been big on instilling anything of value in his niece and nephew; he'd mostly just let them run wild. *The ranch will teach them what they need to know.*

"He had a scar on his forearm."

Parker's arm around her loosened and she felt him shift until his hand closed around hers. The simple squeeze imparted strength to her shaky knees.

Sienna crouched at the hole and ran her fingers along the dirt on all sides. Nothing undisturbed. No loose dirt. "Nothing was buried here."

Parker took the flashlight and circled the room, ten feet in circumference and a rough circle.

Another tunnel began at the far side, but Sienna and Tim had never been allowed to play any farther in than this room.

"I don't see anything, either. The dirt is packed tight. We'd know if you had buried anything here."

Sienna blew out a breath. "I guess we aren't going to find it here."

Parker held out his hand. When she grasped it, he pulled her to her feet and didn't let go. Together they made their way back to the tunnel's entrance.

Sienna could see the disappointment in the slump of his shoulders, but he didn't say anything. They'd thought this was the right place to start, but it seemed she'd led them on a wild-goose chase. If she couldn't trust her own judgment on this, if she couldn't trust the memories she had, how could they possibly solve this problem?

Her shoe hit a rut in the dirt and she stumbled forward. With nothing else to grab, Sienna grasped two handfuls of Parker's shirt. "Sorry."

He chuckled. "It's all right. I need some kind of reason for being here other than as the driver—might as well be to catch you."

She pulled up short. "What are you talking about?"

In the dim light she saw his eyebrow lift.

Sienna opened her mouth but couldn't think of anything concrete. It was just…natural that he was here with her. "Are you planning on leaving if I can't give you a good reason why you should be here? Like dealing with Thomas Loughton wasn't enough."

She'd be hard-pressed to give him a decent excuse aside from abstract need or the fact that no one really wanted to be alone.

Parker shook his head. "Never mind. That was a dumb thing to say. You don't remember what happened, and I shouldn't be punishing you because of it. I'm sorry."

"Apology accepted."

"Just like that?"

Sienna lifted her chin. "Maybe when I get my memory back it'll turn out I'm the one who needs forgiveness." After all, she didn't know why she'd killed their relationship. "If I offer it freely now, maybe you'll do the same when it counts."

Parker stopped at the entrance. Sienna stilled behind him, then whispered, "What is it?"

"I heard something."

He eased to the edge of the mouth of the cave, where he could hear boots on the ground coming up the hill. A diesel engine. The rhythmic rap of a helicopter motor in the distance.

"We have company."

"Should we run?"

Parker thought for a second as he weighed the decision to run for it and risk getting hit by gunfire or stay put and end up being pinned down in the cave.

Neither option was good, but there was usually a better one in these situations. It wasn't like he'd never been in a standoff with his enemy before. Parker was just used to having a team—whether it was SEALs or marshals—to back him up. Sienna had the gun she'd found in the SUV. The bulge was clear on her lower back, under her shirt. He didn't begrudge her the need to arm herself, especially not when it may even come in handy.

Parker grabbed her hand and stepped out. He'd made his decision. He would cover Sienna, and they wouldn't be stuck here waiting for death to come. But it wasn't to be.

Shots pinged the cave entrance beside him and flicked up shards of dirt that rained toward them like hail. Stinging erupted on his cheek, way too close to his eye for comfort. Parker moved them right back into the cave and drew his weapon.

Four men outside gathered in formation to block their exit. Professionals. Hired mercenaries with no personal stake in what was happening, unless he counted the money that would line their wallets when they were finished with the job. That's all this was to them.

Parker scrounged for a way to twist that fact to his advantage. He leaned around the entrance and peered out.

The lead man had a bullhorn. The helicopter rotors spun as it descended to the ground. Dirt and dust circled in the air and whipped up the man with the bullhorn's jacket to reveal extra magazines for his gun. His boots and pants were military but with no designation—like he shopped at an army surplus store.

The man lifted the bullhorn. "Send the woman out, and no one dies."

Parker turned to her. Sienna's brown eyes had widened. Had she remembered her CIA training, it would not have taken away her fear, but she would at least know what to do with it. "That's not going to happen." He gripped her shoulder. "I won't give you up to them."

"Maybe you should. They'll kill you otherwise."

"We don't know that."

He knew she wasn't questioning his skills; she was simply concerned for his safety. The warmth of her care whether he lived or died rushed through him, but there was no time to dwell on it.

"We'll figure a way out."

There was no team within range to help them, but he could call local law enforcement. But would that country sheriff, sixty years old and past ready to retire, live through this? Parker wouldn't be able to stand it if he was responsible for the man being killed or even injured, so he didn't make the call.

He had to find a way to get them out of this all by himself.

"You have two minutes to send out the girl."

TEN

Sienna could see that Parker was torn over what to do. "I'll go." His reaction was immediate as his eyes flashed. He started to talk, but she cut him off. "We shouldn't be arguing about this. There's no time. I'll go with them while you keep searching for the flash drive. It's simple."

Why was he ready to object with her over something that made perfect sense?

"You aren't going out there, Sienna. That's not how this is won."

"It's not a game or some kind of competition."

His blue eyes darkened. "You know what I mean. I won't let you sacrifice yourself. It's not going to happen."

"Okay, hero, how do you expect us to get out of this?" She saw the twitch of his lips. He almost smirked. Almost. "That wasn't a compliment."

"I know."

He had this look in his eye, as though if they weren't in mortal danger, he'd be kissing her right now. Sienna likely wouldn't have protested, but only because she wanted to know if it would bring up any memories of them having done that before. She had no objection to his closeness, and there was certainly attraction there. But when they weren't running for their lives, would they even have anything to talk about?

She folded her arms. "If you're going to object to my plan, that means you have to come up with something of your own. And it had better be good, or the clan of gunmen outside will kill you and whisk me away in their helicopter to be tortured, anyway. But at least I'll know who Thomas Loughton's buyer was."

Didn't that count for something?

Sure, he was used to a mission objective, but it was probably more like a snatch and grab of a person. Terminating the target. Rescuing some victim in distress.

In Sienna's world, it was all about intelligence.

Knowledge was king.

Sienna sucked in a breath.

Parker ignored her minor freak-out and touched the side of her neck. "What is it?" His fingers began a firm massage of the tight knot on the back of her head.

"Thanks." She sighed. "Just a rush of something. More a feeling than a memory, at least for now. But I think things are coming back, because I'm starting to feel a little more like… myself. Instead of feeling like a stranger in my own head."

"Time's up!" The horrible voice boomed so loud it reverberated in her chest like a bass cranked up to ten.

Parker's hand dropped away. "We need to…"

Gunfire erupted outside.

The men yelled. Sienna leaned past Parker to see out, where she saw them scramble for cover. More yelling, and a few broke off toward the source of the shots.

The fast rat-a-tat of automatic gunfire overlaid with the single shots of a rifle. Two men fell, then a third, shot in the back from the other direction.

The man with the bullhorn dove for cover, yelled to his men to get whoever was shooting at them and then ran for the helicopter and safety.

The helicopter exploded. The man flew backward as the fireball launched into the air.

Sienna clapped her hands over her ears to

block out the noise, but Parker grabbed one hand and pulled her. "Run."

They emerged from the cave into the waning light of evening. Had they really been in there a couple of hours? It'd felt like minutes.

"Stay behind me at all times."

Sienna nodded, but he wasn't looking at her. Parker barreled over grass littered with boulders, between trees. He circled debris. How could he even see where he was going? He ran so fast Sienna could barely keep up. If he didn't slow, she was going to…

The grass came up and slammed into her face. Sienna's arm was wrenched forward. She tried to get her legs under her. Parker hauled her to her feet in one sweep. "Come on."

The crack of a bullet echoed through the trees. Then another boom. She tried to run as fast as she could, but what strength she'd had was draining from her into the dirt of her uncle's ranch.

Who had caused this much commotion? Sienna sent up a quick prayer of thanks that someone had. It had to be Nina, because she didn't know of anyone else who knew where they were. Though that hadn't stopped these mercenaries from finding them.

Was there some kind of tracking device on her, or on Parker's SUV? Maybe on one of their phones. But there was no time to look for one now. They had to get to the vehicle and get out of here before one of the mercenaries tried to finish his job.

Sienna scanned the area but couldn't see anyone rushing toward them. "The ranch house." It was between them and the truck. They would have to circle it or run through.

Parker pulled on her arm more and angled them toward the house.

I guess we're going in there.

Parker hit the back porch at a run. The wood creaked, and he flung the door open. When Sienna had cleared it, he slammed it shut and peered out the tall, thin window beside the door. "They saw us."

"Let's hide."

He turned and saw her scurry into the hall closet, yelp and shut the door. From behind it he heard a muttered, "Eew. Don't you come near me, Mr. Mouse."

Parker searched for somewhere to hide, but the kitchen and dining rooms were empty of furniture. Someone had donated or sold everything Sienna's uncle had owned.

He wasn't going to be able to squeeze into the closet with Sienna. It wasn't big enough, and with the adrenaline running through him, he wouldn't be able to be still enough to hide with her without them being discovered.

Footsteps on the front porch brought his attention around. And then voices.

"I saw them."

"Then let's root them out. Otherwise, we don't get paid."

Two men. Parker rounded the corner to the kitchen and pulled his gun, then peered back around. Two men in black fatigues with rifles and body armor, helmets and communication equipment entered the ranch house.

These weren't fly-by-night men; they were professionals. Guns for hire, but good ones who took their job seriously and made sure they were paid enough that they could afford the best equipment.

They cleared the two front rooms and walked down the hall. Sienna had gone silent in the closet. Parker was outnumbered and outgunned but fully prepared to take care of the threat. Her life, and her future safety, counted on him fixing this for her. She only needed the time and space to remember herself. It would be his final gift to her before they parted ways forever.

The first man passed the hall closet; the second three paces behind him.

Parker stepped out, gun raised. "US Marshals, drop your weapon."

The first man lifted his rifle. Parker shot at his vest, knowing he would only bruise the man at best. All they needed was time enough to get to the car.

The man hit the floor and fired back, and Parker dove for cover. He rolled in time to see Sienna swing the closet door open and slam the second man in the face with it. He reared back, his nose already streaming with blood, and brought up his gun. Parker shot again to cover her.

"Let's go."

Sienna nodded and ran for him. Parker got up, and they raced for the front door.

The helicopter was sending a thick column of smoke into the sky, sure to alert locals that something was going on. The sheriff knew they were going to be there. Would he come now? Parker would if it were his town.

As if his thoughts had been heard, two police cruisers crawled up the long drive, the officers on alert. The ranch looked like a war zone.

Parker pulled Sienna around the SUV and hunkered down where the sheriff would see them. He watched the house, waiting for the men they'd subdued to run out after them, bullets flying.

"Good job with the door, by the way."

Sienna turned to him, wide-eyed and breathing hard. "I don't like guns."

"That's not a CIA thing?"

She shrugged one shoulder. "It's not always necessary to kill to get the job done. I'll use one if I have to, but it's not my preference."

Parker's world was a whole lot different. A show of force was often what pushed the situation toward a result. Bad guys would think twice when they knew who he was and what he was capable of.

So often the SEALs were called on to be the world's police, or so it felt. Now that he was a marshal, it wasn't a whole lot different facing down fugitives every day. He couldn't be perceived as weak, or he would fail. And failure meant death.

The sheriff pulled up on the far side of the SUV, between them and the house, as though he was covering them.

When the old man climbed from his vehicle, Parker said, "Two in the house. Armed. Pros by the look of it."

The sheriff smacked his lips together. "Deputy Marshal Parker?"

Parker nodded.

The sheriff's deputy got out of his car and eyed the two of them.

Parker nodded, cop to cop, then turned his attention to the house. "We'll have to let you all take care of this. My friend and I should be going."

The sheriff wouldn't want any help with cleanup, and the farther away they were from here, the safer Sienna would be.

"Stay where you are." The sheriff's deputy lifted one hand, the other on his holstered weapon.

Parker turned to him. "We're fully prepared to provide a statement, but you have mercenary soldiers on this property who need to be arrested. I wouldn't want to hold you both up from being able to do your jobs and keep this county safe."

"Be that as it may…"

"Stan." The sheriff clipped the name short and pinned his deputy with a look. "Let's get to work." He turned to Parker. "I have your number."

Parker nodded, ready to get Sienna out of there. He opened her door for her, and waited while she buckled before he went around to the driver's side.

Why he felt the need to do that, he wasn't sure. Sienna was a strong woman, or she wouldn't have been able to stay calm. He'd rescued kidnap victims before who had fallen apart and wailed all the way to the rendezvous point and drawn every local with a gun to their position because they made so much noise.

Sienna had the good sense to be scared, but she'd remained calm and let him lead them to safety.

But the question remained…

She turned to him as he started the car. "Who shot at all those men and helped us escape?"

"That's a real good question. Nina?"

His face was grim. Sienna didn't know if it was from those men trying to kill them or what. Her fingers shook, so she squeezed them together and tried to still her thoughts. The danger was past, so why did she feel this way? All she had done was hide in the cave and then in the closet. What kind of partner was she? Parker had done all the work…until she'd realized he was going to be killed if she didn't act.

It was only by the grace of God that she'd managed to hit the second gunman with the closet door. She hadn't even known he was going to be there. All she'd wanted to do was distract them long enough for Parker to do whatever he'd been planning.

He was so much more skilled at this than she was. Sure, she knew how to use a gun, and there were some instinctive things she was finding herself falling back on. But mostly all she had was a healthy sense of self-preservation and a few self-defense classes.

"Here." He tossed over his phone. "Call Nina. Find out if she's okay and if that was her back there."

Sienna caught the phone midthought. "We didn't find the flash drive. Should we go back when it's clear and look around some more?"

"Are you sure you hid it there? Could be someplace else, right?"

Sienna shrugged, feeling the weight of the past like a dark cloud in her mind. Why couldn't she just remember? Her own brain held her back and kept her from moving on with her life.

"I have no idea." She sighed. "I just...I have no idea." She gripped the hair beside her face and pulled the strands hard, praying God would give her those memories back.

Parker squeezed the back of her neck. "Give yourself a break. You remembered Thomas Loughton's name, and you remembered playing with your brother. It'll come back. It will."

"I'm sorry." She straightened and saw the confusion in his eyes. "Sorry you keep having to tell me it'll happen. I should know how to be more patient. I've been waiting over a year now." She gripped the phone tighter. "I just get so frustrated."

Not waiting for his answer, Sienna pulled up Nina's number on his phone. Did she even want to know how many women's contact info were stored in his phone? Who was "Hailey," anyway? *Oh wait, that was the woman on his team.* Okay, so she was being dense. She'd been introduced to the woman on the highway after Sienna had almost been kidnapped. Jealousy wasn't attractive in the slightest.

"Hellooo…someone. Anyone…"

Sienna lifted the phone to her ear. "Sorry."

"Yeah, it's been a pretty distracting evening." Nina was out of breath. "You sound okay. How's the all-American hero?"

Sienna smiled to herself, since she'd thought that exact same thing about Parker the night she'd met him. Was that really only the day before? Twenty-four hours and her life had changed irrevocably.

"Well?"

Sienna said, "He's fine." She glanced at Parker, who mouthed, *What?* She shook her head. "We're both fine. How did you know something happened? Was that gunfire you?"

"I have some unique skills, what can I say?" Nina sounded breathy, like she was walking fast.

"You want us to pick you up?"

"Nope." Her reply was instant. "Worry about yourselves, then the flash drive. In that order. I'll be fine."

Sienna sighed. "It's really no problem."

"You pick me up, you draw attention to both of us. Let me cover you. Otherwise, things like tonight are impossible. They'll know I'm here."

Sienna thought for a second. "The men after me, or the CIA?"

"Yes."

"Nina…"

"I said don't worry about it."

"If you think I'm not going to…"

There was a muffled thud, followed by crackling.

A man's voice came on. "I would worry very much."

Sienna froze in her seat. "Who are you?"

"You should remember."

His voice made her want to scream. Slam her fist on the window, the dash. Something. There was something about this man that was pure evil. And he wasn't Thomas Loughton.

This was someone much, much worse.

"What do you want?"

Parker glanced at her, so Sienna turned to look out the window. She had to keep her focus.

The man said, "If you don't know at least that much, then I fear there are more problems than I had anticipated." He sighed, as though she had immensely disappointed him.

"Where's Nina? What did you do to her?"

"Your friend's safety is entirely up to you. Bring me the flash drive in twenty-four hours, and she will go free. The condition she is in will be up to you. Whether she lives or dies is up to you."

ELEVEN

Parker debated as he drove whether they should head back to the ranch and turn the whole place upside down looking for the flash drive or keep on heading out of town. Instead, he called the sheriff and asked about local hotels. The sheriff gave him the number of a bed-and-breakfast about six miles up the highway he was on.

He glanced at Sienna. He'd had her repeat for him exactly what the man on the phone said. Since then, she'd descended into silence. He could see the worry for her friend on her face—a friend she didn't even remember.

Parker reached over and held her hand. Sienna's fingers were cool and tense, but she curled them around his and squeezed as though drawing strength from his presence.

The clock was now ticking on them finding the flash drive and trading it for Nina's life. Though that in itself was full of pitfalls. How did they even know the man on the phone intended to follow through with the deal?

"The man on the phone—was it Thomas Loughton?"

Sienna stared out the window. "My reaction to him felt different. Worse."

He squeezed her hand. She wasn't going to remember by being pressured into it. What she needed...he wasn't sure he knew. The Sienna from two years ago would have fallen back on her faith. Was she doing that now?

Parker pulled up outside the tiny bed-and-breakfast. "Do you want to pray about it?"

She immediately smiled. "Actually, I would."

She kept a hold on his hand as she bowed her head and prayed for Nina. She'd told him before how she felt about prayer. How it gave her peace and comfort to know she wasn't in control and that she could trust and rely on God. The longer she prayed, the more she relaxed. Her words started to flow easier, as though the weight had been lifted from her.

Did he want that for himself? The part of her so devoted to what she believed had always intrigued him. But if Parker did the same, what would he gain? Would he get the peace she had? He had been angry for a long time. First at his ex-wife, and then—truthfully—at Sienna for standing him up.

If he became a Christian like her, what would he have instead? God wasn't going to make his ex-wife suddenly call and apologize. It didn't happen like that. Or, at least, he was pretty sure that it didn't.

When Sienna lifted her head, she smiled so brightly at him that he couldn't help it. He leaned in and captured her joy with his lips. Sienna softened.

Parker touched her cheek and marveled at how soft it was. She was his complete opposite, and yet there was a strength in her that went all the way to a steel core. She was being tested, a trial-by-fire as it were, and he was glad to be the one with a front row seat. He was seeing her as no one else did, and if he were honest, he'd have to say that he didn't want some other man appreciating her. Parker was the one she should be close to.

Forever.

Too bad she'd already decided that wasn't the case. Maybe this kiss would convince her, but that might take a prayer he wasn't yet prepared to say. God was on her side, so how could Parker argue with that? Maybe they already had some kind of agreement going.

Sienna pulled back, chuckling. "I can feel your thoughts going a mile a minute."

He shook his head. "Sorry."

"Don't be. You've been great." She took a breath and pushed it out. "I feel like I've done nothing but fall apart, and fall apart. Now Nina is in serious danger and I'm stuck here with no clue what to do and no memory."

"It's late. Why don't you sleep and I'll keep watch? We'll figure this out in the morning when we've given it some space and thought it all through."

"I'm hoping I'll dream the answer. Or I'll wake up with my memory back."

Parker smiled at her. "That would work, too."

He wanted to know how she felt about that kiss. He didn't like it, but doubts crept in. Parker tried to push them away. Just because she wasn't saying anything didn't mean she didn't like it, or that she thought it was no big deal. Her eyes were as warm and soft as her skin, which only made him want to pull her close again.

But there was a world of people out there and, somewhere in it, more than one man determined to get at Sienna. To get their hands on technology that would make America's defenses vulnerable to attack. Parker had lived his whole life serving his country. He wasn't going to quit now just because he was no longer a SEAL. He would do his duty once more, and maybe even get the girl in the process.

At least until she remembered why she left him.

Parker got their bags from the back, took Sienna's hand and walked her inside the bed-and-breakfast. A slender brunette more likely in her late teens than her early twenties, with dark features and lightly tanned skin, greeted them with a warm smile. "Welcome. The sheriff called ahead. Let's get you folks checked in. I gather you've had a long day."

Sienna chuckled. "You can say that."

The young woman typed on her computer, taking both their names and Parker's credit card for two rooms with a Jack-and-Jill bathroom between. When she turned to get the key from the rack behind her, a tall figure entered.

Parker resisted the temptation to back up. Even with all he'd seen and done in his career as a SEAL and as a marshal, Parker's instinct was to retreat. This guy was bad news.

The man was huge. Taller than Parker with a leather jacket that looked worn and was molded to his slim torso. Under it was a black T-shirt and black cargo pants. He leaned on the door frame and folded his arms. Parker would guess he was midforties, but he could easily pass for a wide age range so he couldn't be sure. The man had the same dark features as the girl, and his dark hair hung over the tips of his ears.

The girl rolled her eyes. "I don't need help, Dad."

The man didn't say anything, and he didn't move.

Dismissing him, the girl smiled at Parker and Sienna, then said, "If you'll follow me, I'll show you to your rooms."

The man in the leather jacket tracked Parker's every step with his eyes, even as Parker hung back and let Sienna follow the young woman. He understood the man's need to protect her, if that's what this was, even as the guy made him uneasy.

He felt the same way about Sienna.

Sienna sat on the bed, alone in a room decorated in floral pastels and tiny china figurines. On any other day she would have looked around, taking in its beauty. Instead, she rummaged in her purse for her phone. Was that how the mercenaries had found them, through their phones? Let them come. If she had any hope of getting Nina back alive, she needed to keep the only link she had to Nina's kidnapper. It wasn't like she and Parker could throw their phones away and go dark.

Parker.

She could still feel his kiss on her lips, the firm softness which correlated so well to his personality. When he'd kissed her, she had been washed away in it, swept up and overwhelmed by a host of emotions she didn't totally understand. Was she remembering? His kiss had felt comforting in a familiar way and yet full of the excitement of a new relationship at the same time. Her head was still spinning from it all.

Despite what had happened, though, Sienna couldn't let Parker's presence distract her from doing her utmost to remember. He would cloud her judgment until she had all the answers.

For all she knew, she could be married. It wasn't impossible. There were reasons she could surmise as to why—if she had a husband—he hadn't come for her so far. The CIA might have been hiding her in Oregon on purpose. Perhaps they'd faked her death.

Sienna could have a child somewhere who didn't know where she was or even that she was alive.

She bowed her head, overwhelmed. *Father*

God, I don't have any answers. Help me find them. Show me the way.

For the sake of her sanity, she couldn't let anything happen between them. Just in case Parker wasn't the man God had created to be her forever love. She believed that was true. She hoped that God might choose to bless her that way. But until she remembered everything, she couldn't be sure that it was Parker who God had brought into her life for that reason.

Taking a deep breath, Sienna called Karen. The woman was involved in her past, and Sienna would be surprised if she wasn't aware of what was happening now. Maybe she could help them or at least tell Sienna something that would point her in the right direction.

Karen picked up the phone. "Yes?"

"I'm still alive, in case you were curious." It had been more than a day, and Karen had always kept close tabs on Sienna. They were never too far apart, even if Sienna had to go into town or if Karen had a meeting. Until now. And the only thing that had changed was that Sienna now knew she was CIA.

"You think I don't care about your well-being?"

She honestly didn't know if Karen did or not. How good of an actor was her former handler? They'd had some kind of relationship before Sienna lost her memory. Friends. Adversaries. Boss/employee. She didn't know what kind.

Karen huffed. "Did you find the flash drive yet?"

Sienna explained what had happened that day, all the while saying a prayer that Karen wouldn't turn around and somehow use the information against them. "He wants the flash drive, or he's going to kill Nina."

"So why are you sitting around in a bed-and-breakfast instead of looking for it? Or is that where you hid it?"

Her insides froze. Sienna glanced around the room as though Karen could see her, sitting there on the bed. "We're exhausted. Rest is the only way my brain is going to relax enough to let something loose."

"So you're basically saying that you have no idea where it is." Karen sighed. "I'm not going to lie. That is very disappointing, Sienna."

"I have to find it, or Nina will die."

"Nina can take care of herself." Karen's voice betrayed no emotion, not even the slightest care for Sienna's friend's safety. "You just worry about getting your memory back and finding that flash drive. I want an identity on who Thomas Loughton intended to sell the flash drive to."

"That's it? You're not going to offer to help?"

"That SEAL isn't pulling his weight? I figured he'd be all over helping the defenseless woman."

"Defenseless?" Hot ire rose up in Sienna. "That's not what this is. He's the only one on my side. It's not like you're rushing to my aid. You only care about the result and not whether any of us get hurt in the process."

"You mean like how I got hurt?"

Was she referring to the drunk driver who had paralyzed her? "I'm not sure what you mean."

Karen said, "I've given this job everything I had to give. As soon as this mission is done, I'm retiring to the nearest disabled-accessible beach, and I don't want to hear from any of you."

Apparently there was no love lost between them.

Sienna sighed. One more reason piled on her to find the flash drive. When would enough be enough? She was drowning under everyone's expectations that she would remember. Nina's life was dependent on her. Every time Parker looked at her it was there in his eyes. He needed her to remember him and to remember what they'd shared with each other.

Karen said a curt goodbye and hung up.

Sienna took a quick shower so she didn't stink up the SUV tomorrow and then pulled on her pajamas. She lay in bed while her mind buzzed around every angle of the problem.

Her thoughts drifted.

The air grew hot. Stifling. Each inhale was like taking a breath in a sauna. Sienna gasped.

"Tell me!" His face was red, gnarled with anger. "I will kill you! Don't think I won't!"

Sienna tried to back up, but she hit a wall. The corner of a door frame.

The edge of the wood bit into her back, laying bruises up her spine. He came at her with a knife then. Sienna struggled for breath against the wet heat that passed for air here. When was her backup going to arrive? She wouldn't make it out of here alive if help didn't come. Thomas was going to kill her.

"Tell me where it is, or I slice you up. And when I'm done, that friend of yours is next."

He knew about Nina? How on earth did he know about Nina? Fear like she had never felt before washed through her, turning her stomach to a roiling mass of sickness.

Should she deny she'd hidden the flash drives? Standing strong against this man was only foolish. He would kill her if she refused to tell him.

The point of his blade pressed the skin under Sienna's chin. His hand was around her neck. Black spots pricked the edges of her vision. His breath was hot on her face. "Tell me where they are."

Someone pounded on the door.

Sienna gasped for breath.

The knock came again. She pushed back the covers and went to the door of the bathroom. The clock by the bed said 03:45 a.m.

Parker's frown was full of concern. "You okay? I heard you yelling."

Sienna sagged like a balloon deflating. "I'm fine."

"Bad dream?"

She trailed to the chair at the desk, turned it and sat. Parker settled on the corner of the bed closest to her. "Wanna talk about it?"

Sienna shook her head. "Thomas Loughton. He was mad, that's all."

Parker crossed to the desk and reached beyond her to get the shoebox. He dumped the contents on the bed and started to look through.

"Do you really think there's something in there that will send us treasure hunting in the right spot?"

He shrugged one shoulder, his back to her as he peered closely at each item. "Can't hurt to look."

This was so frustrating. It was like trying to see a pattern with chunks missing out of it. There was absolutely no correlation between the parts she had, even though they were supposed to go together.

Parker handed her the movie stub. The title of the flick was *Kissing Nina*. Sienna had looked it up and found it was a romantic comedy with predominately bad reviews. Had she really sat through it, or had she gone with Nina just to get a laugh over the whole thing and bemoan the state of their love lives?

"I'm sure it was a bad movie, but I haven't watched it recently."

Parker turned to her. "Look closely at the date and time. And the movie theater."

TWELVE

An hour later Sienna was still staring at the movie ticket stub in her fingers. She glanced out the window of the SUV at the same number, the highway they were on. Dawn had barely broken. Her stomach rumbled. Bad gas station coffee didn't really cut it, but finding the flash drive was more important.

"It's coming up on the left."

The second number on the ticket stub had been painted on the mile marker. The number zero-two came after it. The digits repeated through the time, the highway and the mile marker. What the number two related to, Sienna couldn't figure out.

Parker pulled to the side of the road and she turned to him. "You really think this is for real?" He'd seemed convinced in her room, and he'd driven here like a man on a mission.

"You like puzzles." He paused. "Actually, you said 'treasure hunts.' You're a spy, and you hid something." He shifted in his seat to face her. "I don't think one thing in that shoebox was put there by accident. I think you were intentional with every piece of it, even the photos. Why keep mementos of a life that didn't want you? That's how you described them… your family. The only ones you had left—your parents—are the ones who want nothing to do with you."

It didn't hurt, not when she didn't even remember them or the pain of losing her brother.

Sienna didn't think like most people; that had become plainly obvious to her in the past year. Her closest ally for months had been Karen, who felt more now like an enemy. Those who'd kept themselves apart from her had become close. She hadn't even seen Nina yet, and her friend was the most important person to her right now.

If Sienna had known something was happening, it was reasonable she'd have left clues. Probably for Nina to figure out. Sienna must have been worried she would get caught, and she might not have known she would get amnesia but she had apparently prepared for any eventuality. Now all she could do was thank the Lord that she had left herself a way to find the flash drive, even if it did feel like a wild-goose chase.

"It didn't take that long to get here, and we haven't lost much in trying." Parker's voice was soft, gentle. "It might even save Nina's life. I'm not saying I'm right, but we have to approach this from every angle. Follow every lead."

She didn't argue; she just got out of the car. He shouldn't feel guilty for telling her the truth she'd sought for so long.

Sienna slipped the ticket stub into her pocket and stood by the mile marker. A white post in the ground, it was maybe three feet high with an orange reflective pole that stuck up another four feet—for the snow season. It looked like every other marker on this highway and any other highway.

The ground around it was grass. She knelt and tried to remember if she'd been here before. If she'd buried something here.

None of this felt familiar.

Parker handed her a gardening trowel he'd left the bed-and-breakfast woman a five-dollar bill for.

Sienna didn't think; she just stuck it in the ground behind the wood post and dug. The earth was stiff and hard, but she hacked at it. Parker knelt beside her and used his hands to scoop dirt from the hole.

She sat back on her heels. "How do we know this isn't pointless?"

Parker took the trowel and began to dig.

"We could dig up this whole mountain and we probably still wouldn't…"

The trowel hit something metal.

"Of course, right when I *say* that is the minute you're going to find it." Sienna rolled her eyes.

Parker chuckled as he dug up what she'd buried.

"I don't even remember putting this here. What if it's not ours? What if it's something horrible, and now that we've found it, we're going to be strong-armed by a crusty FBI agent into participating in the hunt for some sicko." Sienna shook her head. "This could be anything."

Parker's chuckle switched to full-blown laughter. "I think you've been watching too many late-night crime shows."

Sienna pouted. "What else am I supposed to do when I can't sleep? At least I can try and figure out who the killer is before the innocent gets captured and the police have to battle to save them before whoever it is becomes his latest victim."

Parker's smile lit up his whole face.

"Okay, so I'm stalling." She blew out a breath. "Open the box."

She wanted to know if this was the end of their search. If they found the flash drive now, Parker would be free to go back to his real life while Sienna kept on trying to remember everything she'd forgotten. Like none of this had happened, and everything she knew hadn't changed in the space of two days.

Parker flipped the box on its side and hit the lock with the trowel until it busted open. The lid hit the grass and a PIN-coded flash drive tumbled onto it.

Sienna didn't move. "Two-six-two-four-six-nine."

"So you do remember."

Sienna stumbled to her feet at the man's voice. He was in front of Parker's SUV. Parker pulled her behind him.

Thomas Loughton stood with his loafers in the dirt pointing a gun at them. He looked like he'd been walking these hills for hours, red-faced and grubby.

"Put the gun down." Parker had his weapon out, pointed back at Thomas.

Sienna reached to the back of her waistband for the gun Parker had loaned her. She came up empty. It was in the truck. She could have kicked herself for leaving it. How was she supposed to help now?

Loughton lifted his chin. "Give me the flash drives."

Parker didn't move, though his brain spun. Flash *drives*? As in…more than one?

Parker glanced down the barrel of his gun at Thomas Loughton and felt Sienna's fingers curl into the back of his belt. He said to Loughton, "Put the gun down and we'll talk about it. Figure out some way we can both get what we want."

Loughton's eyes shifted aside, but Parker wanted the man's attention on him and not on Sienna. The man looked every inch the computer nerd in his khaki pants and light blue button-down shirt, and yet he had strength. He wasn't the unfit, untrained office worker anyone would assume just by looking at him.

"Come on, Loughton. You don't have to shoot us. We have what you want, so let's make a deal."

Loughton narrowed his eyes. "Those flash drives belong to me. Both of them are my property. Give them to me now, or I shoot you. No discussion, no deal."

Like Parker wasn't pointing a gun at Loughton, as well? Apparently the man still figured he had the upper hand.

Parker said, "Put your gun down and I won't have to shoot you when you fire. Neither of us walks out of this if you insist on firing at us."

There was no way he would let Loughton leave. If he got his hands on the flash drive, Loughton would probably shoot them, anyway, for insurance. This battle was going to be mental, at least until Loughton faced the fact Parker was going to do whatever he could to keep himself and Sienna safe.

"Give me the flash drives, and I'll let you leave."

Parker studied him, trying to ascertain if the man was serious or bluffing.

"No. No way!" Sienna's opinion was plain in her voice. She swung around to Parker. "You can't think of giving it to him. We need the flash drive to get Nina back."

That's what she thought of his hesitation? Parker couldn't answer right now. He had to focus on both weapons, even if Sienna's feelings got hurt in the process.

Loughton frowned. "You only have one?"

"How many are there?" Sienna looked baffled.

Loughton stepped forward, which was exactly what Parker wanted him to do. "Then you're coming with me…"

Parker knew what he had planned. The man was going to kill him and take Sienna to find the second flash drive.

"…and we'll find the other one."

Parker launched forward. He sideswiped Loughton's gun away from both him and Sienna, using his left hand. The man dropped the weapon and cried out. Parker followed that with a punch to the diaphragm. Loughton bent forward and gasped for breath.

Parker kicked the gun into the bushes and grabbed the man's hands. He pulled cuffs from the back of his belt and circled the bracelets around both Loughton's wrists while Thomas pulled and struggled. "Enough."

"No!" Loughton fought. "You can't take me in. This isn't an arrest."

"You pulled a gun on a federal agent and you think I'm *not* arresting you?"

"This isn't official business!"

Like that mattered. Still, the question remained unspoken. They were miles—and a state away—from the town where Parker worked, where he knew local law enforcement and could explain what happened.

They were in Nevada now, not Oregon. Where would they take Loughton? Local police wouldn't have a clue as to the caliber of who they were dealing with. Parker and Sienna had one of two flash drives—a fact he almost couldn't believe. Was this really a race to find more than one storage device?

"You can't arrest me. You think some county lockup is going to hold me?" Loughton tried to twist around to face Parker, but he held the man away from him.

"I'll call Karen." Sienna stepped away. "The CIA must have some way of holding him."

Loughton bristled.

Parker yanked on Loughton's cuffed hands as hard as he'd pop a dog leash. He didn't want the man becoming verbally combative with Sienna. He wanted him to ignore her altogether. "I'm the only one you need to worry about right now."

"Until the CIA kills me," Loughton said. "I know that 'Karen.' Don't bother trying to tough it up for me. You're not a bigger threat than that woman. When she finds me, I'll be as good as dead before breakfast."

"Do a deal with me and I'll keep you safe." Parker glanced at Sienna, who had her phone out. She hadn't dialed yet and her attention was on him. He held up one finger and motioned for her to wait. Parker pulled Loughton around. "Karen doesn't have to find you. In return for all the info on the flash drives, on Sienna and on who you were planning on selling them to, I will keep you out of Karen's reach."

Loughton glanced at Sienna then. "You *still* don't remember?" His voice rose in anger. "I risked exposure trying to scare you into re-membering, not to mention the money I spent on that rifle." His voice rose, even as his face reddened. "That would have funded me for a week!"

Sienna stared at Thomas Loughton. They'd been right. He hadn't been trying to kill her when he'd fired all those bullets into her bed-room, scaring the life out of her. "You shot at me so I would remember."

She squared her shoulders, completely out of her element but ready for the performance of her life. "Sounds to me like I should call Karen on the person who nearly killed me."

Behind Loughton, Parker's lips curled up. He gave her a tiny nod of encouragement. It was the only threat she could come up with, given the only thing Loughton seemed afraid of was the CIA coming after him.

"I'm going to take my flash drive and go find the other one." She had no idea where it was but prayed the answer would come to her along the way. "Why should I care what happens to someone who very nearly killed me?"

Aside from Parker's help, all Sienna cared about was getting Nina back. She'd never even met the woman, but the connection of their friendship was deeper than her amnesia. *Lord, keep her safe until I can figure this out.*

Loughton opened his mouth, hesitated and then said, "Don't call Karen."

"Tell me who you were planning on selling the flash drives to."

Parker's face made her wonder if she'd rushed too far into it, too soon. He was obviously going to be better at this. US Marshals—especially ones who dealt with dangerous fugitives all the time, as he'd told her in the car the day before—were probably trained for this kind of negotiation.

He had so many skills, and she had...no clue. Why did he even want to stick around? She wasn't dumb enough to think it was because she had so much to offer. She believed that they'd had something between them. She felt it. Probably it was morbid curiosity over how everything would turn out that kept him here.

Loughton scoffed. "There's no way I'm going to tell you the buyer's identity."

Sienna pulled the flash drive from her

pocket and held it up. "I guess I'll just—" she tossed it beside her foot and lifted her left shoe as though she were going to smash it "—get rid of it."

"No!"

"Once and for all."

"Don't!" Loughton fought against Parker's hold.

"Give me one good reason." She paused. "Other than the fact that you'll lose money."

"If you remembered, you'd know why," Loughton yelled. "It's not my fault you lost your memory."

Sienna pointed to a pinpoint scar on her neck. "Oh, so this isn't from your knife, pressed to my throat while you threatened to kill me and Nina?"

"You do remember!" Loughton renewed his struggles against Parker's grip on his cuffed hands. "Where is the other flash drive? I thought for sure it was at the ranch when you went there, but those mercenaries showed up and everything went wrong." He glanced aside. "You must have been faking us all out. Where is it?" He twisted to look at Parker. "The two of you are going to get the flash drives and sell them on the black market. I knew it!"

Sienna unlocked her phone as she spoke. "I'm calling Karen. We'll be gone before she gets here, but you'll be secure in their custody. A nice care package for the CIA."

Loughton scowled.

Sienna found "Aunt Karen" in her contact list and put it to her ear as though she was listening to it ring.

"She won't let you keep it," Loughton pleaded. "Not even to save your friend."

Parker said, "Then give us enough to go on that we can keep away from whoever these mercenaries you hired are, long enough to find the second flash drive."

Sienna said, "Hey, Karen," into the phone and stepped aside, still listening to Parker and Loughton.

While she said a lot of "Yeah" and "Yep," she heard Loughton say, "I didn't hire those men." He groaned. "The buyer must be trying to get the flash drives by any means necessary, since the sale went south. He's going around me, because I clearly don't have them." He muttered aloud his feelings about that.

"So help me and Sienna get the information before the buyer finds her and extracts their locations."

Sienna didn't figure Loughton cared what happened to her, only what happened to his property. But hopefully he would tell them enough to point them in the right direction, even with selfish motives. She didn't want him to escape justice, and she didn't think Parker would allow that to happen, either. Loughton had to face the consequences of putting all of their lives in danger. If he hadn't stolen the information and offered it for sale, none of this would be happening.

Loughton shoved one shoulder forward, a final attempt at besting Parker physically. Then he said, "Okay. I want an agreement with the marshals. Witness protection, the whole deal. The CIA can't find me, not ever. I get one inkling someone is looking to close in on me, and I'm dust. I'll hide out somewhere no one will ever find me."

THIRTEEN

The helicopter was in the grocery store parking lot when they pulled in. Local police were also there—two cars with flashing lights while the cops kept gawkers back.

Parker let the cops wave him through the crowd of shoppers and parked. He turned to Sienna. "Wait in the car?"

She nodded, a neutral expression on her face that he couldn't read. She'd done well on the highway, enabling him to bring Loughton in to custody. Hopefully, his team would be able to garner enough information from the former NSA agent that they could finish this without anyone getting seriously hurt.

Parker opened the back door and held Loughton's elbow while the man got out. His boss, Jonah, came over and walked with Parker and Loughton to the helicopter. Ames was in the chopper, ready to secure the cuffs to a chain that attached to the floor of the helicopter but had enough slack so Loughton could sit safely and comfortably.

Two paces from the door, the hair on the back of Parker's neck started to prickle. He didn't look around to see where the threat was coming from. He sped up, muscling Loughton faster toward the chopper. "In!"

Jonah knew what that meant. It had happened before, someone trying to shut down their witness. Or kill them so their fugitive escaped custody. Jonah matched his pace, and they hauled Loughton up into the aircraft.

Shots rang out. A circular hole planted in the metal of the chopper six inches above his head.

"Rifle fire." Parker ducked. Loughton and Jonah did the same. Ames aimed out of the window and returned fire.

"Get me out of here," Loughton wailed. "The CIA must have found me."

Crack.

The report was so loud he could hear it over the screams of the crowd as they ran for cover. Police officers yelled for them to leave the area calmly. One called for backup, and another helped a child that had fallen. They ushered everyone toward the safety of the store.

Parker wasn't so worried about them. This was a sniper, not someone who sprayed bullets into a crowd for maximum casualties.

A bullet cracked the window and the pilot cried out. Another shot was fired but didn't hit anything. Jonah jumped in and grabbed a shotgun before he turned back to Parker.

"Wait for backup, or go hunting?"

Parker didn't fancy getting shot crossing the parking lot to search for whoever was shooting at them, but they needed to know who it was. "Hunting."

Jonah yelled, "Ames! The prisoner is yours."

"I'll cover you guys."

Parker nodded. Jonah jumped out of the far side of the chopper. Parker made sure Loughton was going to stay put and then circled wide, past the driver's door of the SUV. Sienna was out of sight, probably hunkered down. *Good girl.*

Jonah would be circling around from the other direction. Eventually they would meet in the middle and have their suspect in custody.

The crack of each shot was evenly spaced long enough for the shooter to reload and aim. Parker had done it himself many times with the SEALs. It wasn't a skill easily forgotten.

He passed the rows of cars until there were no more in the lot between him and the cover of trees in front of the small stores across the street. They were going to have to leave safety and cross the street.

Crouched beside the tire of a rusty beater car, Parker saw Jonah do the same thirty feet to his left. He glanced at the stores, but couldn't see the shooter. Probably on the roof behind a tree. It would limit visibility, but given the distance was less than a quarter mile, a high-powered rifle shot would punch through the leaves and branches like a knife through over-ripe watermelon.

He and Jonah both ran at the same time, and a shot was fired between them.

Parker had to draw the shooter's fire. Jonah was married and had a baby on the way. Parker wasn't going to be the one to tell Elise that her new husband wasn't coming home.

Emergency sirens—police cars—pulled around the corner and sped toward the heli-copter. Good. They needed to finish this clean, without too many people crowding in and making things more complicated.

Jonah ducked into an open coffee shop, probably looking for stairs that led to the roof. Parker eyed the front of the building. Window boxes of flowers. A canvas awning flapped in the morning breeze. A drainpipe. A brick, two-story building with a flat roof.

Parker secured his weapon to the clip on the front of his vest with a snap. He sprinted, leaped and grabbed the drainpipe. He climbed up with his weight braced off the wall and using the brackets holding it to the bricks. The pipe creaked and groaned against his weight, but he just climbed faster.

Crack.

The bullet whizzed past his ear, too close for his liking.

He gripped the edge of the roof, hauled his body over the top and unsnapped his weapon as he landed. Two hands on the grip.

The man dropped his gun and ran.

"Freeze!"

Parker ran after him across the gravel roof.

The siren from an ambulance filled his ears, blocking out everything but his breathing as it tore down the street.

He pumped his legs as fast as he could stand and raced after the man. Medium build, the guy was fast. Short blond hair, drab clothes. He could be easily overlooked. Probably had a face that blended into crowds. Unnoticed.

Parker narrowed the distance a little with every step. The man ran to a door and grabbed the handle. He flung the door open and came face-to-face with Jonah, weapon ready. "US Marshals."

Parker caught up and grabbed the man's arms while Jonah covered him.

Jonah chuckled. "You look winded."

He smirked at his boss. He was out of breath but not unfit. Adrenaline rushed through him from the sprint, but he didn't feel like he'd won the race. "Let's get him into police custody. They can retrieve the rifle."

Jonah shot him a look and held the door open so Parker could take the shooter out first. "In a hurry?"

Uh, yeah. He could admit to himself he was eager to get back to Sienna. She was probably freaked out over what had happened. When this was done, he'd have to take her out for a quiet dinner just to reassure himself that she was good. Stuff like this left a mark on a person, no matter how much training they had or how mentally tough they thought they were.

For all Parker had been taught to do, he had seen and done things that would break most people. They had almost broken him, and he still struggled with lingering nightmares and anxiety that liked to creep in when the team was running down whatever fugitive they'd been tasked to bring in that week. The team knew the signs and how to adjust accordingly when Parker was having a hard time dealing. They had to so that it didn't hurt the job.

But Sienna had none of that. No training that she remembered, and almost no support system.

Except him.

Parker and Jonah walked the shooter and handed him off to the police lieutenant who had arrived. They would need to talk with him eventually, but for now the cops could do the interview and pass on any pertinent information. Ames and Jonah needed to get Loughton to their office to talk over the deal.

He glanced at his SUV but couldn't see Sienna. People were everywhere, cops and EMTs. The helicopter pilot was being bandaged. He turned back to the chopper where Ames was covering Loughton.

He glanced between Ames and Jonah. "If you've got this, I'm going to find Sienna."

Jonah nodded. "Call me if you need anything more."

Parker lifted two fingers in a wave and jogged over to the SUV. Where had she gone? He reached for the door handle and froze.

There was a bullet hole in the cracked window.

He pulled open her door and Sienna slumped out. He caught her, saw the blood and lowered her to the ground.

He sucked in a breath and nearly choked. "I need help!"

Sienna's phone was ringing. When she tried to move, she almost screamed. No sound emerged from her throat, but her whole body curled inward. Her eyes flew open. The sky was a blinding swatch of light, and she blinked, trying to focus.

Parker's face appeared in front of her, along with two other guys. One of whom she'd seen before.

She tried to speak, but no noise came out. She could barely breathe.

Parker touched her cheek. "Easy."

She fought against the rising tide of panic that threatened to drown her. She was all wet. Being held down. She couldn't breathe.

All she could do was choke on the water. The weight on her back kept her under the surface of the bathtub. Information. They wanted information—the location of the flash drives.

She wasn't going to tell them. She'd die before she told them.

Sienna was hauled upright.

Parker. His mouth moved. "Okay?"

Sienna couldn't answer him. A sharp sting pinched her arm and warmth spread through her, a heat that dulled the pain. What had happened to her? All she remembered was that glass had shattered. The car window. She'd ducked as an inferno erupted in her arm. Her shoulder. She'd been shot?

The numbness swept over her, and she was falling.

The man's face was so close she could distinguish the colors in his eyes. Loughton had gone out for food and left her tied up in the hotel room. She hadn't told him where the flash drives were, either. Now the buyer had found her, and he wanted to know, as well.

Nothing but a means to an end. This was what her life had become.

She'd given up Parker and the future she'd seen so clearly with him. A happy future that would have been full of love and family. And here she was, alone again facing a vicious world intent only on their own selfish gain.

Why had she done that? Karen had been so convincing, talking about duty and the life she could have after the job was done. But the job would never be done. Sienna would never be finished. For every evil person taken out, another would rise in his place. It was relentless. The time would come for her to pass the mantle of active intelligence agent along to someone younger, whose passion hadn't waned.

Sienna was ready to give this up, no matter what Karen's best advice was.

The man yelled in her face, odor and mois-

*ture flying at her with his words. Sienna was
forced back below the surface before she could
gasp in a full breath.*

She was going to die.

When she woke, the warm numb feeling was
still there, except for the tube feeding medicine into the inside of her elbow. That pinched.

"Hey."

Sienna turned her head. Her right arm
shifted with the movement and she bit her lip.
Tears filled her eyes. What was she going to
do? She could barely move. Nina was going
to die.

Moisture ran down her face. Parker settled
on the bed beside her injured arm—or was it
her shoulder? She couldn't tell. His thumbs
wiped the tears from her cheeks. He was so
gentle it just made her cry more.

He winced. "I'm sorry. I should have been
with you. Made sure you were okay before I
went after the shooter. I'm sorry."

He was apologizing? She was the one who
had left him at the airport alone. She'd gone
there, even though she wasn't sure why she'd
done it. Karen had known; Sienna was sure of
that. She didn't go anywhere that Karen didn't
know about.

Parker had stood so tall and solid by the coffee shop, sipping from his paper cup. Checking

his watch. Getting impatient. She'd seen when that impatience turned to anger. Then to hurt.

She'd hurt his feelings. But in order to walk away, she'd had to know what it would do to him. She'd needed to know that he felt it just as she did, or else she'd have gone to him. She couldn't have walked away and gone back to work, in serious pain over her decision—even second-guessing herself—if she hadn't known what it was doing to him.

He'd felt their connection, too. Not love; it'd been too soon for that. But what was between them had been big. Big enough that it was a blow to both of them when she'd done what she'd thought was right and walked away.

He looked like he was about to cry. "You're killing me."

Sienna sucked it up. The guilt. The pain she'd caused him. She squashed it all down inside and tried to gain control. Eventually the tears subsided.

Parker leaned down and touched his forehead to hers. Sienna shut her eyes and took in choppy breaths. He leaned back and she mourned the loss. Parker handed her a tissue and she tried to blow her nose in a ladylike way. Which everyone knew was basically impossible. Her face felt all blotchy and hot, but she probably looked even worse.

She glanced at her shoulder for a second before it hurt to strain that way even with just her eyes. Her shoulder was twice the size as normal.

"The bandages make it look worse, but it's pretty mangled and swollen. The bullet went all the way through, but it did some damage. You're going to be laid up for a while."

Sienna shook her head. "The deadline. We have to find the other flash drive and get Nina back."

"My team is on that. Eric and Hailey drove down last night to your uncle's ranch to look around again. They're searching for it there." Parker's voice was soft. "All you have to worry about is getting better."

Sienna shook her head.

"Don't argue with me now." He grinned, but she couldn't return it.

All Sienna could think was how Nina was faring. These people had tried over and over to drown her until she confessed where the flash drives were. But they hadn't succeeded—because she'd fallen into unconsciousness and then woken up with no memory. They were probably hurting Nina for fun.

"I need my phone." Her voice was broken and scratchy, like she'd been shouting for hours and worn it out. No matter how long she'd been unconscious, she had to make sure they didn't hurt…

"Tinker Bell."

Parker glanced back from the drawer by the bed and frowned. "What?"

"Phone." She held up her good hand. That was what she called Nina, because of her brand-new pixie haircut. How had she not remembered that about her friend?

Sienna wanted to cry all over again. Instead, she pulled up her internet search app and typed in all the keywords that she could remember to get her to that awful man who had yelled in her face.

"Bingo."

Parker shifted closer. "What is it?"

"Amand Timenez." A Middle Eastern man was pictured on the screen at a horse race in England.

"Who is that?"

She knew the open question was meant to let her think. She had to give him the answer instead of him pulling it from her, in case he affected her recall of information. "That's the man who drowned me. The man Thomas Loughton was going to sell the flash drives to."

Parker stared at her. "You remember?"

She sifted through her memory. "It's cloudy.

I think some of it came back, but not all. Only the big pieces."

Like Parker.

His face fell. "Okay." He took the phone. "Is it okay if I borrow this? I need to send the information to my team."

Sienna nodded.

Parker stopped at the door. "I'll be back in a minute."

She hoped it was a long one. She'd successfully killed whatever was between them, and it was going to hurt as much to walk away again.

Parker shut the door behind him. Sienna gritted her teeth and sat up. Time would run out for Nina, and there was no way she was going to let her friend die.

She pushed back the covers.

No way.

FOURTEEN

Parker sent a link to the webpage in an email to Jonah. His boss would find out everything they needed to know about Amand Timenez. Parker didn't even want to look at the picture, knowing what that man had done to Sienna. It must have been awful enough to have made her relive her brother's drowning and lapse into a coma. All for two flash drives that would make him money and get a lot of American intelligence agents killed.

Whoever got their hands on the flash drive in Parker's pocket and the one they had yet to find, would have access to the government's database of every covert agency hidden in every country in the world. It would be open season on agents and foreign assets alike. A bloodbath the like of which had never been seen in American history.

And Parker had no intention of letting that happen.

He checked his watch as he strode back to Sienna's room. It was approaching evening, with every minute ticking on Sienna's friend's life. He couldn't imagine how Sienna was feeling, knowing a friend she loved but had never met was in danger. Parker was determined to safeguard Nina's life about as much as he wanted to retrieve the flash drives and get them into the right hands—or destroy them.

Parker jogged the last few steps to Sienna's room and let himself in. "What are you doing out of bed?"

She turned slowly, but her face said it all. She held her injured arm with the other, and her face was pale. Damp lined her hairline. How long until she passed out?

"What do you think I'm doing? Going after the second flash drive. I'm not just going to let Nina die because I'm lying here doing nothing."

He folded his arms. "Recovering from a gunshot wound is hardly doing nothing."

She straightened her shoulders.

Parker stared but knew there was no way she would back down. When Sienna had it in her head to do something, she did it. That much had become clear in planning that first mission with his team the week they'd met. When she wanted something, she figured out how to get it. And—amnesia or not—Nina's safety meant everything.

"Okay, fine." Parker pulled off his jacket, walked over and helped her put her good arm into it. The other side he put on her shoulder. "I'll find you a sling for your arm."

He could see she was going to leave whether he helped her or not. Since he fully intended to help her, he had to make this as easy on her as possible.

To that end, he lifted her into his arms.

Sienna let out a little mew of surprise. "I have legs."

"I know that. But mine are faster right now."

She didn't say anything more.

Parker hit the door handle with his elbow and let them out. He tried not to think too much about what he was doing, or about that lost look in Sienna's eyes. She'd remembered the buyer Thomas Loughton had been intending to sell the flash drives to, called that the "big stuff." But apparently Parker hadn't been an important enough part of her past to be one of the first things her mind recalled.

Not that Parker wasn't glad she'd given him something to go on about who was chasing them. But his heart questioned how important he'd been to her. She'd certainly acted like what they'd had was big—up until she left him standing, alone.

"Are you okay?"

He glanced down at her as he walked past the nurse's desk. He opened his mouth to answer, but was cut off.

"Sir! Sir!" The nurse skidded to a halt in front of them. "What do you think you are doing? That patient should be in bed."

Thankfully, Sienna answered so he didn't look like a kidnapper.

"I'm leaving." The nurse started to object, but Sienna cut her off. "I am leaving. I'll sign whatever I need to sign, but someone's life is in danger and I'm not going to sit around when I'm the only one who can save her."

The nurse had seen his badge. She knew who Parker was, but he hadn't explained Sienna's credentials. The nurse probably figured she was a witness just because he was a marshal, which was fine by him. They needed to stay as low on the radar as possible.

Sienna said, "I'm checking out."

"This isn't a hotel." Still, the nurse bit her lip. "I'll call the doctor."

"Find us a sling, too," Parker said.

He held Sienna while the nurse called the doctor on a cordless phone and brought them the sling at the same time. When she explained to the doctor what they were doing, Parker glanced down at Sienna. Her lips curled up in a smile.

The smile dropped, and she stiffened in his arms.

He turned to look at what had stolen her moment of joy. The elevator was open and three men, followed by Karen, exited. The CIA handler stepped out of the elevator on her feet and not in a wheelchair. The limp in her stride was pronounced, and Parker would guess she couldn't run, but she was walking.

Karen looked both ways. "Find them."

Parker took a step back. Sienna took the sling from the nurse with her good hand, and he said to the woman, "You have my number. The doctor can call me, but we've gotta go."

He turned and strode as fast as he could toward the stair exit.

Sienna gritted her teeth as Parker took the stairs two at a time. He was being careful with her, and it was slowing them down. *God, why did I have to get shot?* She didn't always agree with His plan, but she chose to follow Him, anyway. God knew what He was doing. *Help me save Nina.*

Parker turned the corner at the last set of stairs before the basement. "Sorry."

She didn't say anything. It was obvious enough he was concerned over her injuries. She wasn't going to fault him for it, even though her shoulder burned.

"Almost there."

He grabbed the door handle to the basement parking lot, but hesitated. "Can you shoot?"

With her left hand? "Yes."

He dropped her feet to the floor, gave her his gun and lifted her again. Sienna held it up as he stepped into the basement and looked around for any sign of a threat. She could see the concentration in his eyes and the set of his jaw. There was nothing in the world like watching a highly trained soldier—or agent of some kind—doing what they did best. It had a rush to it, and that was plain to see in Parker. He loved his job. He'd told her as much.

"Why did you leave the SEALs?"

He didn't look down at her. He kept walking, headed for his car presumably, as he scanned the area with every step. "I loved the job, but it takes a toll. I was with the team ten years, hurt my knee. Never did heal right. So I came home and applied for the Marshals. The commute is a lot shorter, and the pay covers all the physical therapy I need."

Sienna smiled, but more out of commiseration than humor. "And here we are. Two aging, on-the-shelf operators."

Parker's chest rumbled with his laughter. He shifted her again and clicked the locks on a new car he'd gotten from somewhere. "Didn't figure you'd want to sit on broken glass. And yes, here we are." He set her feet on the concrete and opened the car door. "Over the hill. Past our prime."

She chuckled at the look on his face. "Okay, so that doesn't quite describe you."

"Or you." He motioned to the car. "Get in. We don't know where Karen or her cronies are. They could be here any second."

Parker helped her settle in the car. Sienna bit her lip. Thankfully, by the time he got in, the dizzy, sick feeling was actually starting to dissipate. Was it going to be like this every time she moved? "Maybe leaving wasn't such a good idea. What if Karen just wanted to talk?"

Parker pulled out of the space and headed for the exit. "There was nothing about her that said 'talk.' She had her war face on, and those men with her weren't your average agents sent to interview the next of kin. Those were trained people."

"So she wants to kill me?" Sienna's stomach would not settle. She glanced around, careful not to shift her shoulder.

Parker lifted a lukewarm water bottle from the cup holder and cracked the seal before giving it to her. "Here."

She sipped the liquid as she spoke. "Or Karen wants to take the flash drive, and we know retrieving Nina alive isn't her highest priority. But it makes no sense that the CIA's agenda is to retrieve the flash drives for themselves and let Nina be burned. It doesn't keep the problem under wraps."

"We don't even know if Karen is working for them for sure, or if she's doing this on her own. She could have hidden you from them after you were injured." Parker hit his turn signal. "Until she does what she intends to do, I'm not sure we'll know. Unless you have some way of calling the CIA and checking in? But that in and of itself will expose you."

Sienna scoured her memories. "I think there is a way to call in, but I can't remember what it is."

"I'd also like to know why suddenly she can walk."

"Not totally."

He nodded. "The limp. I saw that, too. I'm guessing she was injured, maybe even in a car accident, but nowhere near as badly as she made it out to be."

"Because I'll accept a woman in a wheelchair more easily, since she clearly needs her 'niece' in her life." Sienna clenched her good fist. "The amount of times I wanted nothing more than to drive away and never look back, but her 'health problems' prevented me from leaving. It was all a ploy to keep me there."

Parker's hand covered her fist. She loosened her grip and he laced his fingers with hers. "Where do you want to look for the flash drive first?"

Sienna barely knew where to begin. "I still think the ranch has something to do with this, whether it's where I hid the flash drive or not."

"You sleep. I'll drive. We'll be there in no time, and then we'll get Nina back." Parker pulled the ringing phone from his pocket.

"That's my phone."

He handed it over. "It says 'Nina.'"

Sienna hit the button to put the call on speaker before she had time to overthink it. "Hello?"

"Have you found my property yet?"

Amand Timenez's voice was as cold as she remembered. Sienna could picture his face in her head, twisted with rage that she would dare keep the flash drives from him. His pride was such that any attempt made to thwart what he wanted to do was met with nothing less than undiluted rage. She'd met men like that before, but never as bad as him.

Parker held her hand again, and she realized she was shaking.

"We have one of the flash drives."

"And the other?" His voice betrayed no emotion, but she didn't think he had much patience left. Sienna just prayed he hadn't hurt Nina in a way she would never come back from.

She gritted her teeth. It was like she was right back at that moment when he ordered her head held under water and forced her to relive her brother's drowning. A sob worked its way up her throat. "I think I know where it is."

"Every minute it takes you to locate my property is another minute less your friend will be alive."

"Nina isn't part of this. It's between you and me, not her. Let her go. I'll get you the flash drive and you can do whatever you want with it, or me. Just don't hurt her."

She knew it was a bad idea. The more she showed him she cared for Nina, the more leverage Amand had over her actions. With each word, Amand was learning precisely where to put the pressure on Sienna. And how to make it as painful as possible.

"Your friend's life is entirely in your hands." There was a rustle, and then he said, "Tell her."

"Sienna." Nina's voice was a broken sob.

She squeezed her eyes shut and hung her head. "Nina, I'm going to come get you."

Parker's hand squeezed the back of her neck. Nina didn't answer.

"Everything's going to be..."

A scream emerged from the phone. Sienna looked up at Parker as horror swelled in her. What was Amand doing that would make Nina sound like that? Parker grabbed her face, gentle but still hard enough that she focused on him—and only him. His jaw was set, his eyes hard. Imploring her to stick with him, for Nina's sake. It was strength and a promise all wrapped up in one gaze. He would stick with her.

Nina's scream broke off and she started to cry.

Amand said, "You have four hours."

He hung up.

Parker glanced at the dash. "That's eight o'clock tonight. We should be able to reach the ranch and still have time to search before then."

The compassion and solidarity she'd seen in him had disappeared, replaced with a cool efficiency that made Sienna want to cry even as she said, "Okay."

She stared out the window, and Parker left

her to her thoughts. Did he think there was nothing to say?

A distant phone started to ring. She didn't turn but heard Parker say, "Yeah, I'll take you up on that offer. Where's the chopper at?" Pause. "Okay. The closest gas station. Sienna and I need a ride back to the ranch."

A helicopter ride would cut their journey down significantly, giving them more time to search outlying areas of the ranch and still get to Nina before the four-hour deadline—wherever Amand was keeping her.

Lord, don't let her get too badly hurt. She'll let go of trusting You if she thinks that You allowed this to happen to her. Keep her strong. Help her remember You're with her, even in this.

Parker hung up the phone.

Sienna turned to him. "Thank you."

He squeezed her hand again, and she almost smiled. It was his way, using a simple touch to communicate instead of flowery words. And it was more effective than any speech could be. She could trust honest, heartfelt actions far easier than words, which could be deceptive.

He pulled into a gas station and parked at the far end of the forecourt. "They should be here in fifteen. You need anything?"

The pain wasn't excruciating so long as

she didn't move her shoulder at all. "Maybe a soda." Eventually, she would need to get out of the hospital gown, but she'd at least managed to pull on a pair of her pajama pants one-handed at the hospital. She'd assumed Parker had brought them for her because they'd been packed in her bag.

Parker hesitated a moment and then climbed out of the car. He locked it, presumably so no one bothered her, and then jogged across the parking lot. The man never did anything slowly. She felt her lips curl up into a smile. Then she remembered Nina was being hurt and felt hot tears slide down her face.

Her eyelids drifted shut.

The ground was hard dirt and crunchy foliage. Dry ground, parched from the hot summer. Sienna ran, sweat dampening her shirt so that it stuck to her.

Finally she reached the pipe, a white plastic sphere maybe six inches in diameter sticking out of the ground a foot and a half.

Sienna fell to the ground and uncovered it. An old well her uncle had used years ago before he dug a new one closer to the house.

She pulled the flash drive from her pocket, snug in a bundle of paper towels in a sandwich bag that she'd zippered closed. Lord, keep it safe.

She dropped the bag down the well.

The car door opened and Parker got into the driver's seat.

Sienna grabbed his arm. "I know where the other flash drive is."

FIFTEEN

Parker passed Hailey. "You'll take care of her?"

His teammate tapped the side of his arm as she went by him. "I'll sort your girl out, don't worry."

Parker ignored the smirk on her face and walked to Ames. The helicopter had been powered down, but they would need to get going soon.

Ames's eyes were trained over Parker's shoulder. He turned and saw Sienna and Hailey walk into the gas station so Hailey could help her switch out the hospital gown for a regular shirt without hurting her shoulder.

"Interesting woman."

Parker shot his partner a look.

"What?" Ames lifted both hands, palms out. "Both of them, her and that Nina."

"You looked into her like I asked?"

Ames nodded. "I called your friend. Nina

checks out. Moneyed parents who were too busy vacationing in the Med to worry about their child. Nannies, private school. College pretty much paid in full on registration day. Got recruited together with Sienna before they'd even graduated. Internships while they were finishing up. Language training. Stuff like that. After that, it gets a little gray. Career CIA agents, or so everyone thought. Tight, into everything the other one was. Looks like there wasn't much separation in their careers—to the point a couple of times they interchanged identities when one was busy."

"Anything about Nina specifically, like recent stuff?"

Ames said, "The Company hasn't been all that happy with her of late. Seems like she lost her drive for spy work after Sienna was hurt. Suddenly she's flying solo, taking risks. Blowing off missions she's supposed to be finishing. Cutting out early."

"Because of Sienna."

"That would be my guess," Ames said. "That guy at Langley you had me call—interesting character, by the way—he told me 'off the record' that the higher-ups are about ready to burn her. Nina's priorities are skewed, and they don't like it."

"Because she's protecting her friend." Parker

ran his hand down his face. "Nina isn't going to let it slide when Sienna needs her help. Now Amand has Nina and he's doing who knows what while she and Sienna both break. They'll take each other's backs if it kills them. And that's exactly what I'm worried is going to happen."

Ames's face darkened. "There's more."

Parker didn't know if Sienna could take any more. She had been through so much in just a few days. Yes, she had started to regain parts of her memory, but the stress—and now having been shot—was taking its toll.

"Tell me."

The faster Parker could get Nina back and Sienna out of harm's way, the better.

"We got Loughton booked in. Made some calls, got the go-ahead to start talking to him while we were waiting on the paperwork to come through. The attorney's office sent over their guy, and we got to work. Three hours later, we get this call to cease all negotiations."

"What?" The deal was moot, since Sienna had given them Amand Timenez's name, but they hadn't known that.

"Two guys in suits with a court order no one could break waltzed in and removed Loughton from our custody. Loughton is throwing a serious tantrum because he thinks they're taking him somewhere quiet to put a bullet in his head. The assistant US attorney is yelling into his phone and then shuts up like he's getting chewed out, and the two suits go all smug. They walked him out of the building without wasting a second."

Parker laced his fingers behind his head. "The CIA?"

"That would be my guess. I wouldn't be surprised if it was the guys you saw in the hospital with Karen. Though if they'd sent her to get Loughton from the office, then we'd have known she was behind it."

Ames sighed. "When we finally got to the bottom of the court order and found the person who signed it, they said they'd had a break-in during the early hours of this morning and a bunch of paperwork was stolen. We think they forged the court order."

Parker gritted his teeth. "If the CIA, or Karen if she's not working for them right now, has Thomas Loughton, maybe we should be glad. It's one more thing off our plates, one less person to worry about. Karen needs Sienna to find the flash drives, but she also needs to contain this situation. We'll have to be watching our backs."

Amand Timenez was enough. If they didn't have to worry about Loughton, as well, then they could focus their attention. Amand had hired the mercenaries who'd tried to kidnap Sienna from the highway two nights before and the ones who had come to the ranch and tried to take her then. Now he had Nina, and he'd focused his attention on getting Sienna to bring him the flash drives.

The question that Parker needed answering was what Amand would do with Sienna when she brought him what he wanted. He would have no need of her or Nina at that point. He'd shown before that he was capable of extreme violence, which didn't bode well.

Parker would have to make sure both her and Nina stayed alive. And when they were safe, he would stick around long enough to see Sienna's reaction to remembering what went down between them. He wanted to know if she regretted standing him up. He wanted to know if he'd been wrong about her feelings for him, if his radar was actually that far off.

Sienna exited the gas station store with Hailey guarding her. His heart swelled as he watched her walk toward him.

"Man, you've got it bad for her." Ames's voice was full of humor.

Parker didn't reprimand him as he could have. He couldn't take his gaze from Sienna.

He loved her; he always had. But he needed to know if she'd ever felt the same way.

Or if she ever could.

Sienna pursed her lips and blew out a slow breath as the helicopter lifted off. Hailey nudged her good arm to get her attention and then said into her headphone mic, "Parker isn't actually that good of a pilot. He just likes to think he can fly the best. You should probably hold on tight to something."

Parker's laughter echoed through her headset, but his attention was on the windshield. They were headed to the ranch. "I didn't have to teach you guys to fly this thing, but I did. Probably because I'm the best team leader ever."

Ames turned from the front seat and grinned at Sienna. "He just likes to say that because no one else is going to."

Sienna smiled. That was the most she could do. It wouldn't be much longer before she would be unable to block out the pain in her shoulder. Once she used up all her strength and resolve, fatigue would set in. Overwhelmed with agony, her body would shut down.

God, don't let that happen before I get Nina back.

She knew the team's banter was simply to

distract her from her thoughts, and she was grateful. The dark storm of worry was about to drown her in its torrent, and there wasn't much they, or she, could do about it.

Before long, Sienna directed Parker to land in a clearing at the far end of the ranch. Thirty minutes' walk to the house, this was close to the site of the original home her ancestors had built on this land to hide from the sheriff between trips to rob stagecoaches and banks.

Parker helped her down, and she tried to ignore the yearning in his eyes. She knew he thought she didn't remember their relationship, and she had to keep it that way. There was nothing she could do to right what had gone wrong between them, and Parker needed to face that fact.

An engine revved. Parker set her behind him and the three marshals drew their weapons. Sienna had no gun—again. Not that she could do much damage. She couldn't exactly see straight with the pain, and her off-hand shot wasn't actually that good.

The sheriff's off-road vehicle crested a hill and roared toward them. When he climbed out, he strode toward them with his hand on his gun. "You guys want to tell me what you're really here for this time?"

"Sheriff…"

He cut Parker off. "I don't want any thinly veiled truths that tell me nothing, neither. Got me? I want to know what's going on this time, especially considering I did cleanup for you the last."

Sienna peered around Parker's bicep. "No, you don't."

"Not looking so good there, are you, missy?"

Sienna wasn't going to deny it. "We just don't want you to get caught in the crossfire. This was my uncle's land, and I'm just looking for something."

"This 'something' belong to you, or someone else?"

Parker shifted. "Who it belongs to has yet to be determined. We only want to get it out of the wrong hands, and then we can determine if it's too sensitive and must be destroyed or who should safeguard it."

The sheriff nodded. "Those guys you had me pick up that were here earlier, most of them scattered before we could get a lock on them. Pros, if I had to guess."

"That they were."

"Took a shot at my deputy. Winged him like your girl over there."

Not exactly, given Sienna had been shot through and through by a sniper. She was going to have surgery to fix the damage to her shoulder before she would be able to do much more with her arm than twitch her fingers. But what was the point in mobility if Nina was dead?

"I'd like some payback if I can." The sheriff's words were measured. He knew what he was asking.

Parker studied him, which had Sienna studying Parker. What was he thinking? Was he really going to bring the sheriff in on what was happening? More people would just muddy the waters and provide additional targets who could potentially get hurt.

Finally, Parker nodded. "If we can use another pair of hands, we'll let you know."

The sheriff nodded. "Fair enough." He pulled a cell phone from the clip on his belt. "I should be headed…" He tapped the side with the flat of his hand hard enough Sienna winced. "Dumb thing never works. Now I've got no signal." He tapped it again. "That's not right."

Parker shifted and pulled out his phone. Ames and Hailey did the same. "I've got nothing."

"Nope."

"Me, either."

Sienna reached back with her good hand and pulled out her phone. "Mine is fine."

Parker swung around. "Let me see that."

He pressed a bunch of buttons, and then his phone began to ring. He put her cell to his ear. Three seconds later, he hung up on himself. "Your phone has been cloned."

Sienna stepped back. Her reflex to retreat got her caught every single time, and she hated it. It was something she'd never been able to break away from.

"I'll bet it was Karen." Ames seemed sure.

Sienna shook her head. "My aunt?" No, not her aunt. Her head was so muddled. Why would Karen—her handler—clone her cell phone? "She must be keeping tabs on me." She looked at Parker. "On us."

"She probably knows exactly where we are, why we're here and the timeline on the deadline to get Nina back."

Sienna took up where he left off. "She knows I'll do everything to get Nina back. If she wants the flash drives, she'll wait until we have both and then swoop in and take them back before we can trade them for Nina's life."

Parker nodded. "That would be my guess."

Sienna brushed past him and started hiking. It was worth a prayer to thank God for Hailey bringing her socks and sneakers. She felt halfway normal at least, and she was grateful for that. "Let's find it, then."

* * *

Parker didn't like the look in her eyes. She wasn't in any condition to go into battle, though that was clearly what she intended. He followed her to the well she'd described to him and set down the backpack.

He'd had to side trip to a hardware store to get what they needed to bring the flash drive back up to the surface. It was a pretty good hiding spot, and he was proud of Sienna for staying the course of her mission to the end, especially considering what it had cost her.

When it was done, he was going to convince her to quit. If her shoulder didn't count her out of working for the CIA anymore, they had certainly proven they didn't care one iota about either Sienna or Nina. The CIA—or maybe it was just Karen—seemed to only be concerned about the breach of security.

Ames helped him, and they got the scope down the well. The display flickered to life, and Sienna studied the device Hailey held. When they hit bottom, she said, "That's it. It's still there."

Parker assembled the tool to grasp the bag onto the bottom of the winch and tested the mechanism. The claw opened and shut. "Here goes nothing."

He lowered the claw on the winch and used

it to grab the bag. When he pulled it out, he saw the change in Sienna as she visibly relaxed.

"Storage drive?" The sheriff was almost on his tiptoes as he peered over Parker's shoulder to see what all this was about.

"One of two."

"Big deal for a tiny thing."

"Sure is." Parker couldn't explain they held the key to breaching the NSA's security and getting into their computer system. "And we should be going."

He was eager to get out of there before Karen, Amand or anyone either of them might send showed up.

He stood. "Back to the chopper."

They all hustled. Before he climbed in, Parker shook the sheriff's hand. "I've got your number."

"Sure thing."

Ames started up the aircraft. Parker ducked his head and climbed in to sit beside Sienna. Careful of her other shoulder, he slipped one arm around her waist and drew her gently to his side as they began ascending.

"We found them both." The noise from the chopper meant he had to get real close and speak right in her ear.

When she turned to him, he couldn't help but smile. She looked so tentative. "We did."

Parker leaned in and captured her lips with his. "It's going to work out." When she nodded, he went back for seconds. His heart swelled once again at the feel of her in his arms. So right. Like she belonged with him always.

Why couldn't she see what was so plain in front of him? It made Parker want to cry out in frustration. She was fighting what he knew already to be true.

But maybe this would jog her memory.

He smiled to himself even as he kissed her, hoping she would remember them.

"Whoa." Ames's yell broke through Parker's thoughts. "What on…?"

The helicopter jolted.

"They're shooting at us!"

Parker pulled Sienna's seat belt on and then fumbled for his own.

Ames yelled, "Brace!"

The chopper was hit. The engine stuttered and Sienna screamed. Hailey prayed out loud for all of them, and Sienna said, "Amen." Parker couldn't think. The chopper lost altitude, and they screamed again.

"Get us down!"

That was probably redundant, given Ames was already doing it, but their only hope was landing, and doing it in one piece. Going out in a fiery ball of flames wasn't in his playbook. Parker had plenty of stuff to do before he died, and that day wasn't going to be today.

Sienna grabbed his hand, and Ames flew the juddering helicopter to the closest spot he could land safely. Trees collided with the chopper and the windows cracked. An eternity later, Ames yelled, "Hold on!"

The aircraft clipped two trees and slammed into the ground. Sienna cried out and quickly went limp in his arms.

Parker lost the breath in his lungs. "Help us, Lord."

SIXTEEN

Parker coughed and tried to sit up. The helicopter was sideways, and he was lying on Sienna's legs. He shifted off her and brushed the hair back from her face.

Ames moaned, and Parker heard him move. "I'm okay." He paused a beat. "So is Hailey."

Sienna was passed out, so pale she looked dead. Parker didn't want to press two fingers to her throat to check for a pulse—and vowed to himself that he never would. Their future was not going to come to that. Instead, he moved his face down so they were almost nose to nose, and he could feel the small puffs of air on his lips. She was alive.

Parker squeezed his eyes shut.

"How is Sienna?"

"Alive." Parker managed to choke the word out. Had he really prayed in that second before the helicopter had crash-landed? He wasn't the kind of man who felt he needed God's help.

He was trained, capable. But in the heat of the moment, he'd looked to Sienna's Lord to help them all. And He had.

Thank You.

It felt awkward, talking to someone he didn't know, but Parker had to acknowledge his gratitude. They were all alive, and if God had done that, then he was willing to cough up a simple response. He couldn't deny there may very well be something to this "faith" thing.

Parker checked his pockets. He still had both flash drives. Who had shot them down?

He peered out the window but couldn't see much of anything from the angle the helicopter was lying at. The rotors were crumpled, long beams of twisted metal that had been destroyed when they'd tipped onto the ground. Thank God the whole thing hadn't exploded and killed them all.

A man in all-black fatigues with a rifle crept toward the helicopter. A second man appeared six feet to his right, just on the edge of what Parker could see.

The roar of an engine broke through the dull ringing in his ears. A pickup truck pulled up behind the two men. Another man in all black was driving, and Karen sat beside him. The same look she'd had at the hospital was on her face. She was going to get what she wanted, and nothing would stand in her way.

Parker scrambled to his knees and looked around for his gun.

Ames twisted around. "There's no way we can get out without getting shot."

His teammate was right. Karen and her posse would spot them right away.

"That puts us on defense."

Ames nodded his head. "Soon as I locate my cell phone, I'll call in."

Parker located his weapon and pulled his backup out for his off-hand. He crawled toward what was the roof and peered out where the top of the window met the ceiling inside.

Eight feet.

Six feet.

The boom-boom-boom of shots fired echoed out as bullets hit the window. Cracks splintered up and down the tempered glass and Ames yelled, scrabbling around to get in position.

Parker lifted his foot and kicked the window out.

He aimed and fired three shots. A phone was ringing. Parker located the source and saw "Aunt Karen" on the display of Sienna's cell. He put the call on speaker. "What do you want?"

"Come out and we won't kill you."

"Kill me, and you'll never get the flash drives."

Karen didn't even hesitate; she replied immediately with, "I'll order my men to kill the other two marshals first. You can watch. When they're done, we'll kill you. Sienna will tell me where the flash drives are."

"How do you know Sienna didn't die in the crash?" Parker glanced at her. She was still unconscious. Ames was in position, which meant if Parker had to get out and do this deal, his friend could cover him.

"I don't need her. If she's gone, you have no reason to keep the flash drives. They belong to the CIA, and we are the only ones who can safeguard them."

Unfortunately for Karen, Parker could see the pickup and the man beside her. At the exact moment she had spoken so earnestly, the man beside her smirked.

Karen had no intention of turning the flash drives over to the CIA. Whatever she had planned, there were likely more sinister—or selfish—motives at work. And there was no way Parker could let her get to them.

"I'm coming out." He waited a second so either of the men flanking the helicopter didn't shoot him when he stuck his head out.

Parker stowed his backup weapon back in his ankle holster and climbed out feet first.

You helped us before, Lord. Could You help us now? We didn't die. Help me not die now, keep us all safe and don't let the information I carry be used for evil.

Karen stood and climbed down from the cab of the pickup. She stepped aside, but didn't leave the cover of the open door. "Hand over the flash drives and we'll let you live." She motioned to the man on Parker's left, slowly closing the distance between them.

They really assumed he would simply hand them over, no questions asked? Parker had to keep up the ruse that Sienna might be dead, so he shook his head. "You don't even care, do you? And you've been pretending to be her aunt this whole time. How can you be so cold?"

But the question went unanswered.

"Tell me how I'm supposed to get Nina back with no flash drives." He waited, but Karen didn't deign to answer that, either. "Don't you want Amand arrested?"

Karen's cool facade cracked, and she snorted. "The CIA isn't in the business of 'arresting' people. Our methods are far simpler. Faster, and more effective."

"Snatch the flash drives and then order one of your people to take out Amand?" Parker raised his eyebrows. "Is that the plan for Loughton also? Will he be buried in the desert somewhere? Is that why you had him removed from Marshal custody, to silence him so that no one will find out you're trying to get the information for yourselves?"

He folded his arms. "Does the CIA even know you're after the flash drives, or that you spent a year babysitting Sienna just so you could steal them?"

It was all coming together now. The lying. Smothering Sienna every day hoping she would remember where she'd hidden the flash drives. All so Karen could make off with them herself.

Karen rolled her eyes. "Too bad the idiot I sent to get Loughton lost him."

Sienna opened her eyes to find Hailey right in front of her. Hailey pressed her finger to her lips.

Sienna nodded. Her entire body was awash with pain, and she renewed every attempt to push it away before it overwhelmed her.

Hailey held Sienna's wrist with two fingers and stared at her watch. When she let go, she patted the back of Sienna's hand. *Guess I'll live.* Hailey pulled out her phone, called 9-1-1 and, whispering, asked for the sheriff's help.

"Give me the flash drives." Karen's scream was full of rage.

Hailey's head whipped around. Ames didn't

move; his gun and attention trained on what was happening outside, he muttered, "You tell 'em, Park."

Sienna whispered, "Karen?"

Hailey nodded.

She bit her lip and waited for Parker's reply.

"How are we supposed to get Nina back without them?"

"Fake it! I don't care," Karen yelled. "Give them to me now, or I shoot everyone in that helicopter."

"If I give them to you, Nina dies. If I keep them, Sienna and my teammates die." Parker paused. She wished she could see him, to try and read what he was thinking or how confident he was feeling. "I'm supposed to choose who lives and who dies?"

He sounded composed, but was it all for show? *Lord, help keep him calm.*

Karen replied, "The information on those flash drives are worth a hundred of my best agents. But I'll do you a deal." She paused. "I'll give you the fakes we had made up for Sienna. They'll pass muster long enough for you to get Nina back."

She spoke like she was doing them a major favor, being so gracious as to give them the imitations. Replicas that would never be fool-proof despite her claim that they'd enable them to get Nina back. She didn't say anything about the potential problems.

"You expect me to be satisfied with that?" Parker sounded more annoyed than mad. "You think Amand will be satisfied with that? Either Nina or Sienna could die. You want me to choose between them?"

Sienna loved her friend, but if it came down to it, she wanted Parker to choose her and not Nina. Maybe that was the pain talking, or some other deep part of her that yearned to be the one that he wanted. But she'd messed up, and there was no fixing it.

She winced. Her head was a mess. What was she even thinking?

She didn't know why he'd kissed her, as much as she loved that he had. But Parker didn't love her. Not the way she loved him.

The prolonged silence brought her back to reality. Had she missed Karen's answer to Parker's last question? And where was he now? Why could she no longer hear them?

An engine revved, and the sound receded into the distance. Parker appeared at the broken-out window. "Karen and her posse are gone. Now it's time for us to go, too."

Parker helped Sienna up and out of the helicopter. Had that been the right move, giving

Karen the real flash drives? What was Sienna going to say when she found out he only had fakes?

Every inhale he took sent a sharp pain through his side, and he was pretty sure he'd broken the rib that had been cracked from the gunshot the night of the highway. Not the first time he'd broken one, and he doubted it would be the last, either. He surveyed her face. "You okay?"

Sienna shot him a look.

"Yeah, I know you're not. But I can still ask, right?"

Her lips curled up in a small smile. "Yes. Though hitting a pharmacy wouldn't hurt."

If she was in pain and needed something to help, he was perfectly happy to find the nearest drugstore—on any normal day when they weren't crunched for time. "We're cutting it close. We still need to find a ride."

If she hadn't been shot, they would already be headed to rescue her friend.

Ames climbed out.

"Okay?" Parker asked.

"Sure." Ames stretched. "Feel like I got sat on by an elephant, though."

Hailey climbed out, said something under her breath and got a "Hey! That's just mean." Though Ames was laughing.

"Let's get serious, guys. We're nearly out of time."

"I'll call Jonah and tell him we broke the helicopter and we need a new one." Ames strode away.

Hailey glanced from Ames to where Parker stood with Sienna. "I have to…go check… something." She smirked, then walked off and left him alone with Sienna, like this was junior high and he needed to tell her his friend had a crush on her friend.

Parker got Sienna's phone from the chopper. Karen had had the fake flash drives with her. Why, he wasn't sure. But Parker couldn't help wondering if maybe part of her cared— even just a little—what happened to Sienna and Nina.

Amand was determined, but they had to tell him they were ready to trade. Parker didn't want to know how he would react when he discovered the flash drives they had were fakes. But they had to try and get Nina back.

It hadn't sat well with him, giving up their only leverage to Karen—for who knew what purpose. The fakes might be really good facsimiles of the real flash drives, but at the end of the day, they were still pretend and not the real thing.

God, we're still alive when Karen could so

easily have left us for dead. Help us through this, too. You know how dangerous these people are. Keep us safe.

Prayer was becoming more natural every time he did it. Parker listened when Sienna had talked about her relationship with God and how it gave her peace and strength at times when she really needed it. Hope for the future and a sense of belonging when life was seemingly otherwise fine.

To her, God wasn't just someone to fall back on when things weren't going right. Sienna looked to God in the good as well as in the bad. He was her Father. A relationship Parker hadn't understood, or trusted, given his own father's deplorable attempts at parenting. But he wanted to know what it was all about.

"Parker?"

He blinked and focused on her. Should he share the fledgling faith he'd stumbled upon through this crisis? It felt too new to expose to the light of day, like a baby bird struggling for those first few breaths out of its shell. When he had a more solid footing, Parker would share.

Hailey came back over. "Sorry to butt in. Jonah called the local FBI office. It's only a small satellite this far from the city, but they're sending their chopper to pick us up."

"Good deal."

He dialed Nina's number, and a man answered. "You have them?"

"We want Nina back."

"Sienna comes alone and unarmed, or there's no deal." Amand gave them an address. "One hour." He hung up.

"An hour," Sienna said. "Can we get there in time?"

Parker set his palm against the side of her neck and touched her cheek with his thumb. "Let's trust God." He saw the surprise flare in her eyes. "Can you do that with me, show me how?"

Sienna nodded. He'd known giving her a task, even if it was simply being an example to him of what trusting God looked like, would help her focus on the solution and not the problem.

The sheriff arrived first and gave them a ride back to the ranch. Jonah met them there, and this time Parker was the one who flew them to Amand's meeting place. Sienna tried to rest, but it was next to impossible with the thoughts swirling in her head, the pain in her body and the ache in her heart. So she closed her eyes and prayed.

When the helicopter landed, they transferred to a car. Parker helped her walk to the vehicle, her limbs leaden and her head all groggy. She woke again when the car stopped.

Parker turned back from the front seat. "We're here."

Sienna looked around but didn't see anything. "Where?"

"Up at the end of the street."

The address Amand had given them was an old abandoned mansion with a wraparound porch and smashed windows. It looked like the neighborhood kids spent all their free time throwing rocks at the place for sport.

Sienna reached for the door handle.

"Hold up."

Ames handed her what looked like an earbud but without the wire. "The sound quality won't be great, but we should be able to hear enough that if you're in trouble we'll intervene."

But basically she was on her own. Unarmed. Trusting that, if anything did go wrong, they would get there before the bullets hit their target.

Sienna blew out a breath and got out of the car.

Parker climbed out, too. She glanced back and saw him hesitate. What had he been intending to say? He opened his mouth, paused and then said, "Be careful."

"Always am."

* * *

Parker watched her walk away, stunned. That was what she'd said before when they parted. Even though they'd only known each other for a short time and they had been working, she'd had occasion to say it a couple of times, both when she was going into crazy situations. Situations that could so easily have led to him losing her.

It was only when they returned stateside that everything had gone wrong.

He watched Sienna walk up the porch steps and pull open the front door of the mansion. Ames called out of the open car door. "Four heat signatures in the house, Sienna makes five."

"Nina?"

"One is apart from the others. Can't tell if it's her." Ames had a nasty bruise on his forehead.

Parker assembled the plan in his head and then nodded. "You have comms. Hailey, Jonah?"

Jonah got out of the backseat, as did Hailey.

"Let's go." Parker didn't want Sienna in the house too long without cover.

His boss frowned. "Didn't Amand say she should come alone and unarmed?"

Parker stared at him.

Jonah cracked a smile and started to chuckle. "I'll take the west side." He jogged out of sight behind a fence.

Hailey pulled her weapon out. "I've got east."

"Watch your back."

Hailey nodded. Parker unclipped his gun from the snap on the front of his vest and set off toward the house.

SEVENTEEN

Sienna took a deep breath and opened the door. Amand's hair was perfect, his face clean shaven. His Italian silk shirt and slacks were accented by a designer leather belt and shiny shoes. His watch was gold and a gold chain hung around his neck. She'd imagine women the world over would think him handsome. But Sienna knew who he was and what he was capable of.

All she could think about were strong arms that made her want to come close and rest a while. If Parker could ever forgive her for what she had done.

"You're here. Good." Amand clapped.

Behind him, two suited men both had one side of their jackets open, hands on their guns. She recognized both of them now, men who had been in that hotel room when she was tortured. A wave of nausea rolled through her.

Sienna didn't have a vest on, her injured

shoulder prevented it. Not that it would matter. These men would just keep shooting until she dropped, vest or not.

Lord give me the strength to do this. That was all she needed—strength. If she asked for more, she would start to wonder what Parker had wanted to say to her outside. But Sienna had to focus.

"Where's Nina?"

Amand's reaction was immediate. "Where are my flash drives?"

Sienna's head spun as information rushed back to her. Memories, training and mission protocols. Dos and don'ts of espionage. It was a tsunami her brain wasn't prepared for, as though her locked memories simply downloaded the information right when she needed it. Because of the association of being here or for preservation's sake, she didn't know, but she was grateful, anyway.

Sienna reached in the jacket pocket— Parker's jacket.

Amand stepped back. "Whoa."

Both bodyguards pulled out their weapons.

Sienna stilled. "You want the flash drives, don't you?"

He waved one of the guards over with a flick of his finger. "Search her."

Sienna lifted both hands while one bodyguard patted her down. He reached in the pocket she'd been going for and pulled out the two flash drives the CIA had given them to exchange for Nina. *God, please let this work.* Amand took them and turned away. She stepped forward to walk with him, but the bodyguard grabbed her arm.

Thankfully, he hadn't brushed back her hair and checked in her ear. The listening device was crude, but she could hear the team's chatter at low volume as they got into position outside to breach and find Nina.

"Stay."

Sienna could do that, but she wasn't going to be silent. "Bring Nina out."

Amand ignored her.

"Is she even here?" She waited, but Amand simply grabbed the tablet computer from the breakfast bar counter and switched it on. "Is she even still alive?" Dread settled in her stomach. "I want to know where she is. We had a deal."

Desperation swept through her, but she tamped down the physical symptoms and thanked God she remembered how to do that. Amand couldn't know that her need to get Nina back bordered on desperation. She had to play this cool so he'd think she could not care any less. This was business, nothing more.

"Once I have ascertained these are indeed the correct flash drives, you can see your friend."

"At least tell me if she's alive."

He clicked the tablet screen and lifted it to show her.

The room was dark. Nina sat curled up on a dirty bed, just a mattress—no sheets. Her left hand was bandaged and she held it against her with her right.

Years of friendship bombarded Sienna all at once, like a thousand-piece puzzle tumbling to the floor in a jumble. Discordant bits of memory that didn't make much sense except that they came with such a deep sense of longing. Sienna felt a tear drip down her face.

"Where is she?"

The chatter in her ear stilled, then she heard, "Hall is clear. You are go for breach."

Sienna faced down the evil man in front of her, praying Parker would find Nina before Amand discovered the deception.

Amand inserted both flash drives into two ports on the tablet. "PIN code."

Sienna bit her lips shut. This was her last bargaining piece, and she was determined to safeguard her friend no matter what the repercussions were.

"Code."

Had the CIA even programmed it with the same code? Parker hadn't said anything about that when he'd told them what Karen had said and done.

Amand pulled a gun, strode over and pointed it at her.

"If you kill me, you'll never find out what it is."

Parker's voice came in her ear, a terse whisper. "Don't die over this, Sienna. It's not your way to go, and Nina would not want it to happen like this." There was an edge to his voice, an extra layer of longing. It made her heart soar to hear it. Did he really care as much as Nina would if she died?

Sienna would do whatever it took, but she had plenty of life left to live—and remember.

Armand gritted his teeth. "Give me the code."

"Hallway is clear." Parker's voice was all business. Jonah and Hailey checked in, each in turn, confirming they were in the house at the rear and on the other side from Jonah.

Ames came on. "Fifteen feet ahead. Northwest corner." His image only showed heat signatures, not walls.

Sienna said, "Two-six-two-four-six-nine. Now give me my friend back."

Amand sneered. "Not yet."

She wanted to shout at him to get on with this, but Parker needed time to get to Nina and get her out without any of them noticing. After that, it would be down to her to get herself out of the house. Not the first time she'd single-handedly extricated herself from a situation, and not the first time she'd done it for Nina's sake, either.

Amand was at the tablet. He typed the PIN code into both flash drives and Sienna saw the program begin to load. "Bring him in."

The bodyguard left the room.

A minute later Ames said, "A second figure joined the first. They're moving east through the house at a slow pace."

"Got them." Parker's voice was a hushed whisper. "Both male."

Where was Nina?

Sienna stepped forward. "I want to see that picture again."

The second bodyguard, the one who had remained with her, hauled her back to him before she could get more than two paces away.

"So where is Nina?" Ames sounded worried.

Boot steps preceded the bodyguard's return. First through the door was a different man, though, one who looked far worse for wear than the last time Sienna had seen him.

"Thomas." He'd been beaten severely, and his hands were bound in front of him with tape.

"Log in," Amand demanded.

"You think my ID and password are still valid?"

"I know you have others. Log-ins that you made for yourself should the need arise. Don't play me." Amand strode to him and got in his face to whisper something Sienna couldn't make out.

Loughton winced. Then he trudged to the tablet and typed. "There."

Amand grabbed it from him.

Sienna glanced aside. The bodyguard holding her was on the side of her good shoulder, so she could probably elbow him pretty well. But what then? She had no weapon, and three men in this room were armed.

Parker's team chimed in.

"Clear."

"Clear."

"Clear here, too."

Parker said, "Nina is not in the house. The extra body must have been Loughton. Sienna went in there for nothing, and all we have is an image on a screen to work with."

"Get me that tablet," Ames said. "I'll get you their location."

Sienna glanced around the room. She didn't

see how Parker's team was going to get the tablet. Amand pulled out his phone, hit one number and listened. After a few seconds of silence, he said, "I have it."

He hung up and started to turn. In one move, Loughton grabbed the bodyguard's gun, twisted the man's arm under his so that he had both the weapon and the man's arm in his grasp, and fired two shots into Amand.

The bodyguard behind Sienna pulled his gun and fired. Loughton moved behind his man for protection and returned fire. Sienna ran for the front door. Three shots slammed the door in front of her face.

Sienna screamed.

Parker ran for the front room of the mansion. Sienna's scream had torn through him and left his heart bereft of warmth. Whoever had been shooting must have either shot her, too, or hurt her shoulder.

Weapon first, Parker entered the room. Amand and his two goons were both dead.

He heard Jonah and then Hailey enter behind him. Parker strode into the room and scanned the whole place. "Clear."

The front door was open.

"She's not here."

Ames spoke into Parker's earpiece. "I got

them. West off the porch, headed down the street. Loughton is sawing at the tape on his hands and dragging her along."

Parker winced. Sienna had been pushing herself. Eventually she was going to hit a wall, and who knew how much that would set back her recovery. He was pretty sure he'd heard the doctor talk about surgery, but she'd been adamant that getting Nina back was her priority.

Which was fine, considering Sienna's wellbeing and safety had become *his* priority.

Parker hit the front porch at a run, determined to get Sienna back as soon as possible. Who knew what Loughton had planned for her?

"He's got the tape off. Threw it down." Ames sounded like he was running. "I'm pursuing in the car. I'll cut them off."

Parker headed up the sidewalk. He could hear the car engine but couldn't see Ames as he rounded the block to cut off Loughton at the next street.

Jonah spoke over the radio. "The tablet is still here. Cell phones. Hailey and I will try and figure out where they have Nina." He and Hailey were still at the mansion, which meant Parker and Ames had to catch Loughton and get Sienna back before he found transport out of there.

Parker wouldn't have it any other way.

Loughton ran along a path between two houses. Parker gave chase into what looked like a kids' park. He raced across the grass field and saw Loughton up ahead. Beyond him and Sienna was another path.

Loughton sped up and Sienna cried out.

Parker yelled, "End of the line, Thomas."

Sienna's head whipped around, and she stumbled as Loughton dragged her from grass onto the concrete path. She was going to go down hard any minute now.

Loughton kept going. He ran with Sienna down the path to a silver BMW parked at the curb. Amand's car. Had he stolen the keys from the dead buyer?

Loughton flung the driver's door open and shoved Sienna in. He climbed in almost on top of her before she scooted over.

Parker planted his feet and fired two shots into the front tire. The engine turned over and Loughton pulled away from the curb. Parker ran after the car and fired two more shots into the back end, aiming for that tire. But it wasn't good enough. Loughton had Sienna and he was gone.

Ames pulled onto the street just as Loughton reached the end. He screeched to a halt, barely missing colliding head-on with Loughton as he peeled out of the cul-de-sac.

"Go."

Ames was already turning around. "On it. I'll call in."

There was no time for him to pick up Parker. He would lose Loughton if he wasted any time, and they would lose their radio connection if Ames went any distance. He'd be calling local police right now, explaining what was happening and asking for their backup.

There was nothing Parker could do. He stood alone on a sidewalk hundreds of miles from home and prayed. He reached up and grabbed the sides of his head, squeezing. He was completely helpless.

God, we need You. Sienna needs You. Nina needs You.

His earpiece crackled. "I've got something."

Parker spun back toward the house. "Nina?" He jogged across the park to the mansion, where Jonah met him out on the porch. He had the tablet in his hands and Hailey was on Amand's phone.

Jonah said, "I got the IP address of the video call that shows Sienna's friend. I looked it up online, and it's registered to a cellular company."

"A phone?"

"Or a tablet using a cellular connection." Jonah motioned to Hailey. "Shelder's on the phone with the office now. They're calling the phone company to get a location on the connection."

Parker nodded. "Okay. That's good."

If they could ping the phone, they'd be one step closer to finding Nina.

His phone rang. He pulled it from his back pocket, and the screen said "Ames."

"You get Loughton?" He didn't mention Sienna, though she was foremost in his mind. They all knew it. He didn't need to hammer the point home over and over again when they knew his heart was in this.

"Lost him."

Parker gripped the phone. "What happened?"

"I lost him." To his credit, Ames sounded as frustrated as Parker felt over this.

"She's as good as dead now. You realize that, right? Instead of getting Nina back, we've lost both of them and given up the flash drives to Karen in the process."

Jonah stepped closer to him while Ames said, "I'm headed back. The cops put out an alert for the car, and I gave them Loughton's and Sienna's descriptions. If anyone spots them, we'll be the first to know."

Ames hung up, and Parker faced Jonah.

As Parker's boss, Jonah had a great deal of authority over his career and the way he ran his team. But Parker's respect for the man went beyond that. Whatever Jonah was going to say would be earned, and it would be true. But Parker couldn't think what the man could say to fix this.

Parker lifted his hands and let them fall back to his sides. "I don't really need to hear it. Just tell me how we're supposed to find Sienna when we have no idea why Loughton took her or where they went."

Hailey hung up and spun around. "I got a location on the friend. It's not too far from here."

Jonah didn't move his attention from Parker; he just lifted one eyebrow.

Parker ignored it. "Let's go."

He strode down the porch steps and watched for Ames to come back with the car. While they waited, he thought through what had happened. "What about Loughton? Did he have a phone?" Sienna would have left hers in the car when she went in; she wouldn't have taken it in the house where it could have been discovered and used against her.

Hailey got on her phone again. "I'll find out."

Ames drove up and they all climbed in. While Hailey called the office and asked for information on Loughton that might give them a phone number they could trace, Ames glanced at Parker in the front passenger seat.

After the fourth glance, Parker said, "What?"

"It wasn't my fault." Ames paused. "I know you care about Sienna, but I'm sorry. A minivan pulled out in front of me, windows down, full of kids. I wasn't going to slam into the side and risk seriously hurting them. As it was, I scraped the back bumper."

"Fair enough." Parker knew Ames well enough to know his usually joking exterior hid a big heart. Not that Parker would have made a different decision, but Ames was wired a whole lot differently. The man's career as a homicide detective before he'd transferred to their team had left him with deep scars.

He gritted his teeth. "Let's just find Nina and pray that somehow we figure out where Loughton took Sienna."

Jonah reached forward and squeezed Parker's shoulder. The man had rededicated his life to the Lord a few months back. Sienna believed in the Lord. If it was going to help get her back, he would do whatever it took.

Or he would die trying.

EIGHTEEN

Sienna huddled in the backseat, watched street signs and traced the route they'd taken. Loughton drove like a crazy man, but apparently no one cared. The streets were almost completely deserted, the sun having dropped behind the houses and set. Streetlights lit the main roads in whatever town this was; she didn't know what it was called.

"Why did you take me?" Sienna didn't move her attention from the streets outside the car window, but she had to get him talking if she wanted to find out the answers to all of her questions.

"Why not?" Loughton was out of breath, but the tone of his voice was that of a man who thought he'd won. "You ruined everything, and I'm going to make things right. I planned this meticulously. I gave up my whole career to retire and live the sweet life, and you just had to come along and mess up all of it."

"It's my job."

Loughton laughed. "The CIA, systematically messing up men's great plans the world over."

Sienna much preferred the Bible verse that said God directed man's steps, despite what they had planned. He was sovereign.

A rush of peace filled her. It calmed her racing heart and helped her breath to even out. God was in control, as He had been all along. The mission. The coma. Nina's future. Sienna's guilt and pain over what had happened with Parker. God had His hand on all of it, and she didn't have to worry.

Thank You, Lord. She breathed. *Now if You could help me get out of here, that would be great.*

She smiled to the window, despite the situation. God had proven Himself to her before, and she was sure this situation would be no different.

"I don't know why you're smiling, being as you're going to die. You're only going to live long enough to see me win, and then I have no use for you. Unless you can think of a way to make my life sweeter."

Sienna looked at him so he knew exactly what she thought of that idea.

Loughton laughed. "Too bad."

When he looked back at the road, she glanced around. There was nothing on the floor or the seat. She'd already tried opening the door while they were driving away from Parker. If Amand had brought Loughton to the mansion in his car, Loughton would probably have known the child locks were on in the back. Which she figured was why he'd pushed her between the seats into the back instead of letting her sit in the front passenger. That had hurt.

Then Sienna saw it. The side of Loughton's jacket was flipped up onto the space between the front seats, where the cup holder was. In his pocket was a cell phone. His, or someone else's that he'd stolen. Who knew? But it didn't matter.

Sienna was going to steal it.

"I'm sorry Amand brought you into this." Maybe appealing to the fact that Amand had him beaten before she got to the mansion would help. Loughton's pride probably didn't like the fact that he'd been bested and then forced to log in to the NSA's system using a dummy account that hadn't been suspended.

Loughton scoffed. "Karen was going to have me killed before Amand's people snatched me from her assassin. Now I'm free of him, and

I have the flash drives. So far, it's better than being dead."

"I don't know. My shoulder hurts pretty bad."

Loughton laughed and got into a turn lane. Sienna leaned forward while he said, "Serves you right," and pickpocketed his phone.

Sienna pressed the button to unlock the phone and nearly cried out in frustration. It was Loughton's phone—the picture of his daughter on the lock screen was proof enough—and it wouldn't unlock without his thumb swipe.

How had he got it past Amand's men? Or had he simply picked it from a dead man's pocket before they left the mansion? She'd seen him grab the flash drives, and something else.

Either way, there was no way she could call for help except to dial emergency. She should call the police, but would anyone believe her? She wanted to call Parker. He could get the police to her with more urgency, given his pull as a marshal. She quickly came up with an alternative plan and prayed it worked.

The light turned green. Loughton hit the gas and careened through the intersection. Halfway through the turn she reached forward with her good arm and pulled up the hand brake. Before Loughton knew what had happened, she slammed his head down onto the steering wheel. He cried out and let go of the wheel.

Sienna prayed they wouldn't hit anyone, grabbed his hand and used his thumb to swipe the phone.

Loughton pulled the car off the road and slammed into a concrete bench with a roar. He twisted and came at her between the front seats with a determined look on his face. He spied the phone in her hand and made a grab for it.

Sienna reared back. Had she just lost her only opportunity to call for help?

Loughton was going to kill her.

Ames slowed the car as they passed the house where they suspected Nina was being held. The phone that was being used for the video connection had been traced to this house.

Parker assessed the entry points in front. *God, help us get her alive.*

They parked around the corner, outside another street. TVs flashed in the front windows of houses, people who hadn't yet gone to bed even though it was late. Otherwise, these were working people tired after a long day.

There was no reason to gear up, given this was the second breach of the night. All they needed was extra ammo. Back-to-back raids weren't unprecedented, but usually they weren't personal like this one was.

Parker said, "Let's go."

Technically, Jonah was boss, but it was Parker's team and they'd all worked together long enough it wasn't like anyone would get confused as to who was in command.

"Hailey and I will take the back." Jonah and Hailey broke off.

Hailey had taken the time to call her daughter and speak to her husband, their other teammate Eric, who'd had to head back home. Parker admired her ability to sign off the call and switch back to the operation and the objective. He'd known SEALs that weren't able to leave their personal lives at home when they went on a mission.

Parker crept up to the front door under cover of darkness. No lights were on downstairs, and the curtains had been drawn on the upper level. It was an ordinary three-bed house any small family would live in. Certainly not like the place anyone would stash a hostage. Although, that was likely the point.

Ames stood to one side of the front door, Parker to the other. Ames gave him a nod. Parker said, "Breach." He kicked in the front door and they went in.

No furniture. Empty rooms.

Jonah's voice came over the radio. "Kitchen is clear. Cell phone on the counter and an empty pizza box. Recent."

Parker noted the smell more than anything else. No one had opened a window in months, and the air wasn't moving at all. "Living room is clear."

"Downstairs is clear." Ames led the way upstairs.

They broke off at the top of the stairs and both opened different doors at the same time. Hailey and Jonah had stayed downstairs to provide cover in case someone came home. The place was practically deserted. Was Nina even here?

Parker entered the bedroom.

Ames said, "Bathroom is clear. I'll check the…"

Parker cut him off. "She's in here."

Sitting on a dirty bare mattress in the corner of the room, huddled against the wall, Nina lifted her eyes. When she saw who it was, they narrowed. "You."

"The one and only." He stowed his gun and moved across the room to her. Parker wanted to tell Sienna that he'd found her friend for her. That they'd done it. "Loughton took Sienna."

"The buyer?"

"Amand Timenez and his men are dead."

"The flash drives?"

"Karen has them."

"That's not good." Nina's voice was quiet. She held a bloody kitchen towel to her that was wrapped around her left hand. "Not good at all."

"Can you walk?"

She nodded. Parker helped her to her feet and supported her weight as they crossed to the door. Ames stood at the top of the stairs. "House is clear."

His gaze fell on Nina and his eyes flared. His mouth opened, but he didn't say anything. Mr. Smooth had no words, faced with an injured, admittedly beautiful woman. She did bear a resemblance to Sienna. Parker could have laughed aloud at his partner, floored by a woman for the first time in his life. Or so far as Parker knew.

Ames recovered enough to say, "Does she need an ambulance?"

"No ambulances." Nina shook her head. "I'll take care of it."

Ames frowned. Parker shot him a look. If the woman didn't want this to be officially reported, that was her business. Parker wasn't going to argue, and he wasn't going to let Ames push her. Not when Parker needed Nina to help him find Sienna.

When they got to the bottom of the stairs, Jonah introduced himself and Hailey. Ames finally stuck his hand out to Nina, and said, "Wyatt."

She grabbed it with her good, right hand but didn't manage to hide the wince.

"You're certain you don't want someone to look at that?"

To Ames's credit, she did look very pale. Her skin was clammy, and Parker was concerned about the wound being infected.

Instead of answering, Nina turned to Parker. "What are you doing to get her back?"

"Finding you."

It sounded so lame when he said it out loud, but what other choice did he have? "We lost the car they were in. Local police are looking for them, and we're checking into Loughton's background to see if we can ascertain where he might be taking her."

"And you think I know where she might be?"

"Finding you was the most important thing to Sienna, and I've done that, even though she's not here to see it. Now I need you to help me find the only woman I've ever loved."

"Okay."

Parker blinked. "Okay?" He wasn't surprised she'd do anything for Sienna, but had this experience opened Nina up to accepting Parker in her best friend's life?

Nina shrugged one shoulder. "I'm a tough CIA agent who happens to secretly be a pushover for a good love story." She cracked a smile.

Parker grinned. Ames's trademark laughter filled the room, making everyone grin. But it was short-lived.

"He's going to kill her."

Nina nodded. "He's going to kill her."

Parker's phone rang.

Sienna gripped the phone while Loughton roared. He clutched his head where she'd kicked him.

"Parker."

"It's me," she gasped.

"Where…?"

Sienna cut him off. There was less than no time. "West Haven Street and Forty-third."

Thankfully, the car crashing hadn't drawn too much attention, given the late hour. But someone was out there. Would they help her?

"We're on our way. Just sit tight, okay?" She heard shuffling, and then he yelled, "Get me a location, too. I'm not making a mistake with this."

Sienna relaxed a fraction. But she couldn't get out of the car. So long as Loughton was in the front seat, she had no way out. Even if she incapacitated him, could she get between the seats to climb out? Likely not with her shoulder screaming at her like this.

"Just hurry."

She could hear him running. Meanwhile, Loughton was recovering quickly. He reached over to the front passenger seat and grabbed something. Sienna realized what it was even before Loughton pulled the trigger.

"Sienna!" Parker's voice rang through the phone.

Sienna screamed and kicked at Loughton's arm. He yelled, the gunfire stopped and the gun dropped to the floor by her but too far away to reach down and get it.

Loughton launched himself between the seats and tried to grab for it. She kicked his hand. His arm. He cried out. Sienna kicked his head and he fell backward. Loughton's head collided with the dash where the radio was. She sucked in a breath and he slumped back.

"Parker."

"Are you okay?" His voice was steady, solid.

Sienna whimpered. Pricks of light flashed at the edges of her vision.

"Sienna?"

She opened her mouth, but no words came out.

"Sienna, talk to me. Are you okay? Please be okay. Sienna? Don't die. I love you. I have since the first day we met and it didn't go away, even though I could have hated you for not coming to the airport, for choosing your job. But I don't blame you. You had the right to make that choice, and it hurt but I understand."

It was the wrong choice. Sienna should never have believed Karen knew better. She should have trusted her heart. Trusted what she felt for Parker and the connection they had. God had put him in her path for a reason, and she had to believe that reason was for her good. Just as it was for Parker's good.

God, help him to trust in You. Help Parker to believe what I believe. It'll make it easier for him if he doesn't get here in time. She gasped. *Help him get here in time, Lord.* If he didn't, it would destroy him. Sienna knew, because she would feel the same way if he died.

"I understand because I love you, Sienna."

Though she'd given him no answer, he continued, "You're the best thing that ever happened to me, and that's never changed...and Nina's scowling at me. I guess she still doesn't think I'm good enough for you, and that's fine.

I won't ever be good enough for you. But I want to spend every day showing you why I'm the right choice. If you'll let me."

What was he suggesting? Sienna couldn't believe he simply swept away what she'd done. He'd forgiven her. Or at least that's what it sounded like. Parker had let go of the pain she'd dished out to him. Was that because he'd surrendered it to God?

She wanted that for him, because Sienna knew what it meant in her life. Peace. Joy. The ability to forgive herself because she had been forgiven of so much.

"Parker." His name was a whisper. Did he even hear it?

"Sienna." He exhaled. "Thank You, Lord."

Joy filled her heart, even as she slumped farther down in the seat. Darkness crept in. Blue and red flashing lights lit up the inside of the car, but she couldn't respond. All Sienna could do was fall into the well of unconsciousness.

For the hundredth time, Parker said, "Drive faster."

Jonah had his attention on the GPS map on his phone. "Take the next left. We should be there in two seconds."

Parker saw the police cars. The lights and sirens. A handful of officers were crowded around the car Loughton had taken. How he'd driven that far on a low tire was anyone's guess. If there was any breath in him now, Parker felt like squeezing the last of it out. At least until he knew Sienna was completely safe.

He flung his door open before Ames had even stopped their vehicle and got out as soon as he could. He hit the ground at a run and raced to Loughton's car. The closest cop put out one hand to stop him, and then saw Parker's badge and let him pass.

He jogged to the car, where an officer had the door open and was helping Sienna out. Loughton was lying on the ground being looked at by officers, and two EMTs were making their way over.

Parker waved over the closest officer. "That man is extremely dangerous."

The cop nodded and immediately reached for his gun, covering his fellow officers and the EMTs who were to treat Loughton. Thomas shifted as he regained consciousness.

Sienna moved her legs out the car door and Parker supported her so she could stand.

An SUV turned the corner and pulled up. Four people got out and flashed ID badges. "Thank you, we'll take it from here."

Sienna whispered. "They're CIA."

NINETEEN

The back door of the car Parker had been in opened. Sienna sucked in a breath as Nina exited the vehicle. It was her. She knew it. She knew her friend, now that she remembered everything.

Sienna completely ignored the approaching CIA people and moved to go to her friend but stumbled. Parker reached for her. He held her gently, his strength evident in his touch. It was exactly what she needed, and she felt the tears prick her eyes.

Two EMTs intercepted Nina, and Ames stood with her. The police had to be baffled, given they'd been called there because of a kidnapping involving the CIA and US Marshals, and no one was saying anything.

Parker rested his hand against her cheek. "Are you okay?"

She shook her head. That was the honest answer. It had been a crazy few days and she needed a week to recover—most of that probably in a hospital bed. She'd done what she'd had to do. Now it was time to rest.

Parker leaned close and touched his lips to her forehead. "You will be." He sounded so determined it made her hiccup a sob. He was going to try and fix everything. And she knew why now.

He wanted to be the one to save her once and for all. An idea that made her heart soar just thinking about it. There was a lot to clear up with the CIA, but she wanted to follow where God had led her...to Parker. To a future with him of God's design. A wonderful adventure that had nothing to do with the past and everything to do with love and forgiveness.

The two CIA agents in the lead reached them, and Parker moved to stand in front of her right shoulder, guarding her. Sienna took his hand with her good one and squeezed a thank-you. He returned it, so she leaned her head on the outside of his bicep. The CIA had to see that she looked awful. It wasn't a ruse to make them sympathetic to her. She needed doctors, medicine and probably surgery.

"Sienna Cartwright?"

She nodded. It was good to know she was right; she didn't know these men personally. She only recognized the badges...and the swagger. Probably she would always wonder if there was something she had forgotten.

"We need you to come with us."

"For what?" Parker didn't sound impressed at all with what they were trying to do. It made Sienna want to smile.

The CIA agent flicked him an unimpressed glance. "Ms. Cartwright is required to debrief. She will be given the medical attention she needs. We take care of our own."

"Let's do that first." Parker waved over one of the EMTs and tugged her in that direction so she was several paces away from the CIA agent while the EMT lady whistled.

"Rough day, huh?"

Sienna smiled. "You could say that."

She glanced aside to where Parker had gotten in the CIA agent's face and was talking in a low tone she couldn't make out. What was he saying to the man?

The EMT touched her shoulder, and she winced. "Gunshot?"

Sienna nodded. Parker glanced at her. She wanted to be talking to him, and maybe he could touch her cheek again. That had been nice.

"Looks like it's already been treated for the most part, but you should still go in and see a doctor. I can see how much it's hurting. Anything else I should know?"

"Just bumps and bruises."

"Okay. I'll believe you, but you're coming in." She put her arm across Sienna's shoulders but didn't add any weight to her back.

Sienna started to walk and saw Nina push away from the EMT treating her. Sienna's friend shot the CIA agents a look that said everything Sienna needed to know on how she felt about them.

They met in the middle. The EMT with Sienna stepped back a couple of paces so they could have some privacy.

Nina's blue eyes bored into her, a gleam there that anyone else would have missed. "You forgot me." She clutched her bandaged hand to her chest.

"I forgot everyone and everything. I had amnesia."

Nina's eyebrow lifted. "That's hardly an excuse for forgetting your best friend."

Sienna lifted her chin. Nina had taught her to not back down for anything, to take the hits life dished out and keep on punching. "You'll have to forgive me, then. Since that's what best friends do." Sienna motioned with her chin to Nina's bandaged hand. "Did Amand cut off your finger?"

"He tried." Nina scrunched up her nose. "Turns out it's not that easy."

"Ouch."

Nina cracked a smile. "Kind of like getting shot in the shoulder." She stepped forward. "You think we can hug one armed?"

"We can try."

Sienna closed her eyes and soaked up the deep friendship of years of knowing someone, sharing everything and going through all of life's major changes together. The bond between Sienna and Nina would never be broken.

"Thank You, Lord."

Nina shook with a chuckle. "Amen, sister."

Sienna pulled back. "I'm done with the CIA."

"Me, too." Nina glanced in Ames's direction. "The real world is looking pretty good right about now."

Sienna looked over and saw Ames staring right back at Nina. She glanced at Parker, who had his gaze on her. He looked ready to punch the CIA agent. She felt the grin curl up her mouth. "It really is." She looked at Nina again. "Let's retire."

"Deal."

Parker watched Sienna embrace her friend. He wanted to go to her but was faced with getting this CIA agent—who'd introduced himself as Alan Barnes—to go easy. Both Sienna and Nina needed serious medical attention.

He crossed the stretch of asphalt between them to where the two friends seemed to have come to some kind of agreement. "Sienna…"

"Ms. Cartwright." It wasn't the CIA agent, but one of the police officers who'd been at the scene first. "We'll need an initial statement from you before you head to the hospital."

"She needs to sit down." Nina's voice invited no argument.

"Agreed." The EMT began to lead Sienna toward the waiting ambulance. Loughton had already left, a detail of two officers riding with him.

"I'm coming." Nina walked with them.

The officer started to ask Sienna questions. She glanced back and gave Parker an apologetic smile. At least now he knew she wanted to talk with him as much as he wanted to talk with her. They would get their chance.

Soon, Lord. Please.

It was becoming more natural to speak with God the more Parker did it.

"We need her debriefed."

Parker turned.

"This is a matter of national security, and no one is going to get in the way of our nailing down exactly what happened the past few days." Barnes folded his arms. "Especially with regards to Karen Miller's involvement in this matter."

"You don't want to just ask me where the flash drives are?"

"You know about those?"

Parker rolled his eyes. "I exchanged them for two fakes."

"You did what?" Barnes went pale. "Who has them?" He lifted the clear plastic bag Sienna had put them in. "And what are these?"

"Those are the CIA's fakes they had made up to trick Thomas Loughton and Amand Timenez two years ago." He flicked his finger toward them. "Karen...you said her last name was Miller? She has the real ones."

Barnes turned to the man next to him. "Find her."

The agent scurried off to one of their vehicles.

"What else?"

Parker walked the man through what he knew. Karen's plan for the past year, what she'd told Sienna. Everything that had happened since that night on the highway. All of it up until this moment.

CIA agent Barnes strode away, pulling out his phone as he walked.

Ames walked up beside Parker. "Nice guy."

Parker felt one corner of his lips pull up. "Sure was."

But Parker didn't want Barnes to commandeer Sienna for the time being. Even with her in the hospital, there would still be endless questioning by the CIA and local police until this was all ironed out. Eventually she would be free to take a break and—hopefully—they could talk some before she went back to work.

Jonah strode over. "Hailey, Wyatt and I have to get back to the station." He clapped Parker on the shoulder. "We can't all be on vacation like you."

Parker laughed. "Yep, the past few days sure felt like a holiday break."

Ames grinned. "You realize that hauling-yourself-up-the-drainpipe maneuver is going to go down in history. Not to mention your little speech on the phone." Ames switched his voice to a high pitch. *"I love you, Sienna. I always will."*

Parker swung his arm to cuff Ames around the neck but slow enough the man could duck. He did, even though he knew Parker wasn't trying to hit him.

He glanced at Sienna.

Jonah said, "Boy, I remember that feeling."

"Huh?" Parker turned to him.

"Being in love. Those days when it's all fresh and new."

Parker couldn't help smiling in Sienna's direction. "Yeah."

"Understandable." Ames looked at the two friends. "Perfectly understandable. It's actually good to know that Mr. Tough Guy has a heart and not just the cold hard rock we all thought was there. I mean, you have to admit you were pretty bitter. But none of us knew why or who did you wrong." He grinned. "Guess now you're all fixed up." Ames clapped his hands together. "Who's next?"

Jonah clapped Ames on the shoulder. "You're the only one left."

Parker figured they were getting a little ahead of themselves, considering Sienna hadn't even told him she felt the same way or acknowledged the fact he'd forgiven her for leaving him in Atlanta. He understood it now, but he needed to come to an agreement with her that they had some kind of relationship they could either settle into or start working on.

But Ames and Jonah were right. He'd told the truth on the phone. He did love her.

"If you know anything of her location now, if she said anything about what she had planned or where she was going, we need to know."

Sienna gave more of her weight to the EMT, and the woman braced but held her up. "If I knew, I would tell you."

The CIA agent—Barnes—said, "You lived with the woman for a year."

"She was in a *wheelchair*." Out of the corner of her eye, Sienna caught Nina fighting a grin. "And I had amnesia. I wasn't exactly looking for inconsistencies in her story."

"You had amnesia?" The EMT shifted to feel around Sienna's head. "Did you hit your head today?"

"No. My head is actually fine."

"We'll keep an eye on it, anyway."

Sienna said, "Great. Let's head out. Nina?"

Her friend laughed. "Only you could be funny when we're in this much pain."

The pain was considerable, but Sienna had a lifetime of practice putting off what she wanted in order to get something done. A lifetime of meeting other people's goals, their expectations, their qualifications for success. Nina was the one exception, never demanding anything of Sienna other than what she demanded of herself. They'd pushed each other to succeed and picked each other up when they failed.

And now there was Parker. He'd wanted her future, and she hadn't been ready to give it up. But the reality was that in order to say yes to him, she only had to give up other people's expectations for her and exchange them for the life she wanted for herself. The secret dreams she'd always had.

"You can come with us," the CIA agent said. "We'll get you to one of our hospitals where you'll be treated properly."

The EMT jerked straight. "Say what?"

"We're already going to the hospital." Was the man slow or just so determined he couldn't see straight? "I've told you everything I know. Give me your card in case I think of anything else, and I'll be able to call you. Isn't that how it works?"

"Not in the CIA."

"Then I'll just call you when I'm recovered. Thanks and goodbye."

"You aren't going anywhere without an official escort." He waved at one of his friends. "In the ambulance, please."

The man nodded and climbed in.

Parker strode over, his anger directed at the CIA agent. "I've told you that you can do this later."

"There is a debrief procedure in place for a reason. No one simply walks away from the CIA. We've been watching you for two years. We have to know why this happened now.

Who else do you think is going to clean up the mess you've all made?"

Sienna rolled her eyes.

The agent turned to Parker. "As for you, you can fully expect charges to be brought against you for turning sensitive information relating to national security over to an unknown."

"Karen? Seriously?" Parker scoffed. "If you've been watching, where were you? Why didn't you step in and help?"

"The CIA doesn't operate on national soil. This should have been kept quiet and dealt with in-house, but we're required to amend protocol in real time."

"Which is an official way of saying you sat around doing nothing, didn't help, let four people die and swept in afterward to do the cleanup on *your* mess. All so you could save face in front of whoever you report to."

Parker shook his head and turned to the ambulance. "Make some room. I'm coming, too."

The EMT shook her head. "No more. We're full."

Sienna opened her mouth to object, and the EMT stuck her with a needle. She coughed. "Ouch."

"I think you forgot you're scared of needles."

Sienna said, "Now that you said that, I am!"

The EMT shook her head and tsked. "And to think I was impressed. Now I find out you're a baby about needles."

Sienna gasped. "I am not..."

The woman patted her on the head. "Lie down and rest, dear."

Nina looked in stitches trying not to laugh aloud. Sienna shot her a look. Parker stood at the open door and she reached out to him. "Save me. They're all crazy."

He smiled. "Anytime. Any place. I'm there."

"Aw."

Sienna glared at the EMT. It was hard, because the room was starting to spin. "He told me he loves me."

The EMT chuckled. "I have no doubt."

Sienna looked back at Parker. "I don't want to be a CIA agent anymore."

"I don't want to have this conversation when you need to sleep."

She frowned. "You don't?"

"Rest," he said. "We'll talk later, okay?"

"You're not mad?"

Parker shook his head. "Why would I be mad?"

"I love you, too."

He smiled. It was very handsome.

"Thank you."

Sienna said, "You're welcome," even though she didn't really know what for. Everything was getting fuzzy. She really did need to sleep. Maybe for a week.

"Parker!"

He grabbed the ambulance door before it closed and found Nina behind the EMT.

"Thank you," Nina repeated her friend's words.

"For what?"

She shook her head. "Coming to get me. For saving her. For loving her. For getting her to admit that she loves you… Do you want me to continue, or is that enough?"

"That'll do it." He grinned. "And you're welcome."

"Are you coming to the hospital?"

He nodded. "I'll be right behind you guys. If Sienna wakes up, tell her I'll be right there."

Nina nodded. She glanced at the CIA agent with a tinge of worry in her eyes.

Parker didn't blame her; faced with people she wasn't familiar with when she'd recently been kidnapped and almost had her finger cut off, he'd feel the same. If Sienna's friend needed a little reassurance, he was okay with it.

"I'll be right there."

The door shut, and Nina left with Sienna and a CIA agent.

"Need a ride to the hospital?"

Parker turned to Ames. He thought he was coming, too? "Taking the rest of the day off?"

"I was thinking more like the weekend."

Parker held out his hand for the keys. "This time I'm driving."

TWENTY

When Parker arrived at the hospital, he'd discovered Sienna was never admitted. It took him six hours to track down the EMT, who told him the CIA had stopped them halfway there and escorted both Sienna and Nina into their custody—and their car. The EMT had called for police backup, but the CIA had been gone with the two women before the cops got there.

That was three weeks ago.

Parker had called in every favor and pulled every string he had to pull from Oregon to the Naval Air Station in Oceana but he'd found no trace of Sienna or Nina. They'd disappeared off the face of the planet.

Parker had gone from shock to anger to prayer to hope to a waning desperation. Now all he had was numb cold, a feeling that had him sitting in his truck outside the house where Sienna had lived with "Aunt Karen" for a whole year before he'd even spoken one word to her.

A year of wasting time, wondering what she was doing. What she was thinking.

Lord, where is she?

His team had tried to help or to commiserate with him on the outcome just in case she never came back. But what had kept Parker going was navigating his new faith. Asking questions and searching out the answers. It hadn't brought Sienna home yet, but it had given him some semblance of peace to be able to rest in the Lord.

A shadow moved behind the curtain.

Parker cracked the door on his truck and strode over. He tried the front door. When he found it unlocked, he went inside.

The furniture was still there, as were the belongings he'd assumed were supplies more than personal. The CIA—or maybe just Karen—had outfitted the cover with enough so that Sienna would believe it, or at least not ask too many questions.

He stood in the foyer and listened.

A rustle.

Parker pulled his weapon and strode down the hall. Sienna's bedroom door was cracked, but whoever was in there didn't want a light on for their business—just the ambient evening light from outside.

He eased the door open. "US Marshals. Stop what you are doing and…"

It was Sienna.

Parker choked on his words. She was there. Black slacks and a light blue blouse, her long hair falling in yellow waves around her face. Her left arm was in a sling, and in her other hand she had a folded shirt. An open suitcase lay on the bed.

"Going somewhere?"

"Put your gun away and I'll tell you."

Parker stowed it in the holster on his belt.

"I'm packing up."

"Were you planning on saying goodbye?"

She hadn't moved much, those telltale signs he saw all the time in witnesses and people with something to hide. She was good enough Parker couldn't read her at all.

"I hadn't decided yet." She turned and flipped the lid closed on the suitcase before she slumped down beside it. Parker could see signs of fatigue in the lines on her face. "I just…" She sighed, her eyes downcast. "I hadn't decided yet," she repeated.

He wanted to ask her why she was hesitating, why she now doubted what he'd said to her. It was still true. As far as Parker was concerned, nothing had changed from that accident site three weeks ago.

Unless something was different for her.

Parker walked over and crouched in front of her. His knee popped and they shared a smile. He surveyed the sling on her arm and the edges of the white bandage he could see on her shoulder. "How are you?"

"The surgery was more extensive than they thought. It'll be a while before I can use my arm like normal again."

"Physical therapy?"

She nodded.

He'd had enough injuries to know that had to seriously hurt. She was probably battling the pain every day.

"Sienna?"

"Yeah?"

"I still love you."

Her eyes flared. It was the only consideration she gave to any kind of reaction. "I still love you, too."

"That's a good place to start, don't you think?"

"Start what?" She glanced around the room. "I'm not who you think I am—I never was. The CIA agent in me has acted without remorse for the good of the mission. I don't want to be her now, but she is part of me. That Sienna, the one they want to come back, will always be inside me."

"You think I haven't done things I later regretted in the heat of battle? I have plenty of things I'd like to take back, including not coming after you when you didn't show up in Atlanta. I shouldn't have let you go. I should have found you and convinced you that we work."

"I was there. I had to see you, but I also knew I had to let you go."

"That was then," Parker said. "This is now. A new day. A new life."

"Do you believe that?"

"I do." He scanned her face and saw the worry there. The concern. Did she think this wasn't going to work? Sienna hadn't had much of a family life, but she couldn't deny that when they were together it had been right. Parker wasn't going to risk their future this time. He was going to do everything in his power to make it so.

For both their sakes.

Sienna had spent the past three weeks—minus surgery—talking through every single mission of her entire career. Every victory, every failure. Then on to every interaction with Karen and finally what happened between Parker pulling up behind her to the car accident with Loughton.

Karen had been located by a joint task

force that included the NSA and the FBI and
brought in. She was currently being detained
on charges of espionage. The CIA—or whoever won that fight—had the flash drives.
Nina had been stitched up and was back at
the condo, considering a move to this side of
the country. Sienna couldn't wait to see her
friend full-time again.

If she didn't have to tell another story for a
year, it would be fine with her.

"I want a normal life now."

Crouched in front of her, Parker looked so…
accepting. Something that had been in short
supply in a life where Sienna had to prove
herself over and over again. Where she'd had
to fight for everything. Friendship. Respect.
Parker was offering her everything she had
ever wanted with no work whatsoever.

He smiled. "I'm glad to hear that."

"No more CIA."

"If that's what you want to do."

What did she want to do? She'd enjoyed taking care of animals. Tending to her small farm.
But was it a life plan?

Sienna glanced around the room. "Do you
know why I picked this house when Karen and
I moved here?"

Parker shook his head.

"I was searching online. Karen told me we'd

sold our old house, and I knew where I wanted to live. The town seemed so familiar, even just looking at maps. Now I know that's because you told me so much about it, and the way you talked it was obvious you love it here."

She paused long enough for him to nod. "I know why. I picked this place for the same reason. It's home—exactly the type of place I could see myself spending years. Waking up, drinking my coffee on the back deck. Watching kids play on the swings. There aren't any now, but I would put some in..."

Parker laid his hand on hers. "Who owns the house now?"

She'd paid in full three weeks after she woke up from the coma. "I do."

He looked around, much like she had done. "It's a great house on a great piece of land. Definitely one I could see raising a family in." He paused. "So long as I married the right woman first." His mouth curled into a grin.

Sienna couldn't help but return it. "Who might that be?"

Parker reached in his coat pocket and pulled out a ring. "I bought this before we were supposed to meet up in Atlanta."

Sienna gasped and put her hand over her mouth.

"Not that I would have asked you to marry

me at the airport, but I don't think it would have been long after. I knew, even back then."

"So did I," Sienna admitted. "I just lost my way in the days we were separated. I started to believe Karen when I shouldn't have listened. I should have followed my heart." Her breath was coming in sharp gasps now.

Parker sat on the bed beside her and drew her into his arms. Sienna rested there, more at peace than she'd ever been in her life.

"The past is in the past, Sienna. It's gone. There's only us now and the promise of what can be." He leaned back and touched the sides of her face. "Today is the start of all our tomorrows. And it's not going to be perfect, but I'll stick with you and we can work on it together. As a team."

Sienna was already nodding. How could she say no when her heart was so full of love? She'd come here to pack, thinking there was no way they could be together. But Parker had loved her through everything. Why not through the rest of her life, too? Doing the same for him was going to be no hardship.

Sienna lifted her chin and smiled. "Yes."

* * * * *

Dear Reader,

Thank you for joining me on this journey with Sienna and Parker. The idea that we can love one another despite past hurts is something God has been writing on my heart for years. And it's a beautiful story. His love covers even the worst of sins, and He still continues to pour it into us because it's who He is. All we have to do is ask, and God will show us His love.

Neither Sienna, nor Parker, were perfect. Just like you and me. Both of them needed to let go of what had happened in order to embrace the future. My prayer is that you and I will be able to do the same thing anew, every day.

I hope you enjoy my books. Thank you to those of you who have written to tell me. My website address is authorlisaphillips.com, where you can find out about upcoming novels and contact me.

I would love to hear from you.

May God richly bless you,
Lisa Phillips

LARGER-PRINT BOOKS!

GET 2 FREE
LARGER-PRINT NOVELS
PLUS 2 FREE
MYSTERY GIFTS

Love Inspired®

Larger-print novels are now available...

YES! Please send me 2 FREE LARGER-PRINT Love Inspired® novels and my 2 FREE mystery gifts (gifts are worth about $10). After receiving them, if I don't wish to receive any more books, I can return the shipping statement marked "cancel." If I don't cancel, I will receive 6 brand-new novels every month and be billed just $5.49 per book in the U.S. or $5.99 per book in Canada. That's a savings of at least 19% off the cover price. It's quite a bargain! Shipping and handling is just 50¢ per book in the U.S. and 75¢ per book in Canada.* I understand that accepting the 2 free books and gifts places me under no obligation to buy anything. I can always return a shipment and cancel at any time. Even if I never buy another book, the two free books and gifts are mine to keep forever.

122/322 IDN GH6D

Name _____ (PLEASE PRINT)

Address _____ Apt. #

City _____ State/Prov. _____ Zip/Postal Code

Signature (if under 18, a parent or guardian must sign)

Mail to the **Reader Service**:
IN U.S.A.: P.O. Box 1867, Buffalo, NY 14240-1867
IN CANADA: P.O. Box 609, Fort Erie, Ontario L2A 5X3

**Are you a current subscriber to Love Inspired® books
and want to receive the larger-print edition?
Call 1-800-873-8635 or visit www.ReaderService.com.**

* Terms and prices subject to change without notice. Prices do not include applicable taxes. Sales tax applicable in N.Y. Canadian residents will be charged applicable taxes. Offer not valid in Quebec. This offer is limited to one order per household. Not valid to current subscribers to Love Inspired Larger-Print books. All orders subject to credit approval. Credit or debit balances in a customer's account(s) may be offset by any other outstanding balance owed by or to the customer. Please allow 4 to 6 weeks for delivery. Offer available while quantities last.

Your Privacy—The Reader Service is committed to protecting your privacy. Our Privacy Policy is available online at www.ReaderService.com or upon request from the Reader Service.

We make a portion of our mailing list available to reputable third parties that offer products we believe may interest you. If you prefer that we not exchange your name with third parties, or if you wish to clarify or modify your communication preferences, please visit us at www.ReaderService.com/consumerchoice or write to us at Reader Service Preference Service, P.O. Box 9062, Buffalo, NY 14240-9062. Include your complete name and address.

LILP15

REQUEST YOUR FREE BOOKS!
2 FREE WHOLESOME ROMANCE NOVELS
IN LARGER PRINT
PLUS 2
FREE
MYSTERY GIFTS

HEARTWARMING™

Wholesome, tender romances

YES! Please send me 2 FREE Harlequin® Heartwarming Larger-Print novels and my 2 FREE mystery gifts (gifts worth about $10). After receiving them, if I don't wish to receive any more books, I can return the shipping statement marked "cancel." If I don't cancel, I will receive 4 brand-new larger-print novels every month and be billed just $5.24 per book in the U.S. or $5.99 per book in Canada. That's a savings of at least 19% off the cover price. It's quite a bargain! Shipping and handling is just 50¢ per book in the U.S. and 75¢ per book in Canada.* I understand that accepting the 2 free books and gifts places me under no obligation to buy anything. I can always return a shipment and cancel at any time. Even if I never buy another book, the two free books and gifts are mine to keep forever.

161/361 IDN GHX2

Name _____ (PLEASE PRINT) _____

Address _____ Apt. # _____

City _____ State/Prov. _____ Zip/Postal Code _____

Signature (if under 18, a parent or guardian must sign) _____

Mail to the **Reader Service:**
IN U.S.A.: P.O. Box 1867, Buffalo, NY 14240-1867
IN CANADA: P.O. Box 609, Fort Erie, Ontario L2A 5X3

* Terms and prices subject to change without notice. Prices do not include applicable taxes. Sales tax applicable in N.Y. Canadian residents will be charged applicable taxes. Offer not valid in Quebec. This offer is limited to one order per household. Not valid for current subscribers to Harlequin Heartwarming larger-print books. All orders subject to credit approval. Credit or debit balances in a customer's account(s) may be offset by any other outstanding balance owed by or to the customer. Please allow 4 to 6 weeks for delivery. Offer available while quantities last.

Your Privacy—The Reader Service is committed to protecting your privacy. Our Privacy Policy is available online at www.ReaderService.com or upon request from the Reader Service.

We make a portion of our mailing list available to reputable third parties that offer products we believe may interest you. If you prefer that we not exchange your name with third parties, or if you wish to clarify or modify your communication preferences, please visit us at www.ReaderService.com/consumerchoice or write to us at Reader Service Preference Service, P.O. Box 9062, Buffalo, NY 14240-9062. Include your complete name and address.

HW15

YES! Please send me **The Montana Mavericks Collection** in Larger Print. This collection begins with 3 FREE books and 2 FREE gifts (gifts valued at approx. $20.00 retail) in the first shipment, along with the other first 4 books from the collection! If I do not cancel, I will receive 8 monthly shipments until I have the entire 51-book Montana Mavericks collection. I will receive 2 or 3 FREE books in each shipment and I will pay just $4.99 US/ $5.89 CDN for each of the other four books in each shipment, plus $2.99 for shipping and handling per shipment.*If I decide to keep the entire collection, I'll have paid for only 32 books, because 19 books are FREE! I understand that accepting the 3 free books and gifts places me under no obligation to buy anything. I can always return a shipment and cancel at any time. My free books and gifts are mine to keep no matter what I decide.

263 HCN 2404   463 HCN 2404

Name	(PLEASE PRINT)	
Address		Apt. #
City	State/Prov.	Zip/Postal Code
Signature (if under 18, a parent or guardian must sign)		

Mail to the **Reader Service:**

IN U.S.A.: P.O. Box 1867, Buffalo, NY 14240-1867
IN CANADA: P.O. Box 609, Fort Erie, Ontario L2A 5X3

* Terms and prices subject to change without notice. Prices do not include applicable taxes. Sales tax applicable in N.Y. Canadian residents will be charged applicable taxes. This offer is limited to one order per household. All orders subject to approval. Credit or debit balances in a customer's account(s) may be offset by any other outstanding balance owed by or to the customer. Please allow 4 to 6 weeks for delivery. Offer available while quantities last. Offer not available to Quebec residents.

Your Privacy—The Reader Service is committed to protecting your privacy. Our Privacy Policy is available online at www.ReaderService.com or upon request from the Reader Service.

We make a portion of our mailing list available to reputable third parties that offer products we believe may interest you. If you prefer that we not exchange your name with third parties, or if you wish to clarify or modify your communication preferences, please visit us at www.ReaderService.com/consumerschoice or write to us at Reader Service Preference Service, P.O. Box 9062, Buffalo, NY 14269. Include your complete name and address.

MMLPBPA15

READERSERVICE.COM

Manage your account online!

- Review your order history
- Manage your payments
- Update your address

> ### We've designed the Reader Service website just for you.

Enjoy all the features!

- Discover new series available to you, and read excerpts from any series.
- Respond to mailings and special monthly offers.
- Connect with favorite authors at the blog.
- Browse the Bonus Bucks catalog and online-only exculsives.
- Share your feedback.

Visit us at:
ReaderService.com

RS15